THE

Orphan

BRIDE

BRANDI GABRIEL

TO MY LORD AND SAVIOUR, JESUS CHRIST
I never could have done it without You!

One

August, 1883

Lucy Weber glanced back at Mrs. Walton and strengthened her resolve. She had to do it. There was no way out. She took a breath and shut her eyes.

Please, God, help me with this. I know that this is all in Your hands, Lord, but please, please let her agree with me. You know I am terrified about this. I just can't imagine...

She swallowed hard. There was no need for her to get emotional about something that might not even happen.

Please give me the strength to face my future, no matter what it is. I'm trusting in You, God. Don't let me down.

"Lucy?" a young voice whispered beside her.

She opened her eyes. "Yes?"

"Were you praying?" Joan asked in her sweet, raspy voice.

"Yes, Joan. I was."

The little girl looked up at her with big, trusting eyes.

"I'll pray too. I don't want you to go."

Lucy battled the lump in her throat. "Neither do I." She kissed the top of the five-year-old's head. "You keep praying, okay? I'm gonna go ask her."

Joan gave her a brave smile and nodded her encouragement.

She sighed deeply to calm herself but it proved useless. Attempting to stamp out the butterflies in her stomach, she stood. She walked down the train aisle to the seat that Mrs. Walton, who was presently looking at the newspaper, occupied. The woman continued to read, either not noticing Lucy or simply ignoring her.

Lucy had the distinct feeling the latter was the case.

She cleared her throat.

Mrs. Walton spoke without lifting her attention from the paper. "Why are you up from your seat, Lucille?"

"I, um, I wanted to talk to you…about…something."

The portly woman raised a brow and finally turned her gaze to Lucy.

"May I?" She motioned to the vacant seat beside Mrs. Walton, who nodded her consent.

She sat, watching her hands idly smooth her dress, then glanced up at Mrs. Walton. "I, um, well I was…"

"Lucille, you know I despise mumbling. If you have something to say then say it, but if not, go back to your seat and leave me alone."

Lucy forged ahead. She only had one chance. "I do have something to say, ma'am. I was…I was wondering if maybe you needed a partner. To help with all the orphans. You know, helping them behave and act proper. I-I've become friends with a lot of them and they really listen to me, if you've noticed."

"I've noticed."

"Well, I was hoping that maybe you'd be pleased with my work and let me, well...let me, um, stay on and help you? Instead of getting off. I know I'm that age but I really think I could do better here. Please? I would love to help you."

Mrs. Walton sighed. "I knew that was it. Several young women like yourself have asked me the same thing before they were let off. I have to give you the same answer I gave them."

Lucy's hopes sank.

"You are very talented with children. You are. But you know the rules. When you turn fifteen, you're off. There's nothing I can do to stop it."

"I know," she said quietly. She felt sudden pressure at her hand and glanced up in surprise. Mrs. Walton never showed affection to anyone.

"From every child that has come through, you have been the most helpful. Out of all of them. I truly am sorry, dear. But there's nothing I can do."

Lucy nodded and quickly stood, not wanting to show the tears threatening her eyes. "Thank you, Mrs. Walton, for your time." She went back to her seat.

Joan looked up at her with hopeful eyes. "What'd she say? What'd she say?"

"She said no."

The little girl sagged back against the seat, her lower lip trembling as tears pooled into her eyes. Lucy forced a smile, shoving back her own emotion, and pulled Joan onto her lap. She smoothed back her hair and spoke into her ear. "Don't worry. Maybe someone will want to adopt you and we'll live at the same place."

Joan lifted her head. Her wheat blonde hair stuck to the moisture on her face. She sucked in air through her nostrils. "Do you think so?"

"I'll tell you what. When we get there, I'll ask my new husband to adopt you. All right?"

Joan nodded, then snuggled against her. Lucy held tight to the little girl she considered as family. Out of all the children that had come through the orphan train, Joan was the one that clung to her.

She remembered seeing the traumatized toddler sitting at the orphan drop. The child's clothes were ratty and torn, hardly hanging on the baby's too-skinny body. She stank as if she'd crawled out of a refuse pile and her hair was nasty and stuck together in hard clumps. She had scrapes and bruises on her face and limbs. They couldn't get her to say a word for three days. All she'd done was cry. Cry, eat, and sleep. Since the little one didn't seem to know her own name, Lucy had named her Joan after the warrior Joan of Arc.

And Joan had clung to Lucy, who was the only one old enough and willing to take care of the deprived child. The girl's dependence on her had once cost her a home. A family had been willing to adopt Joan but she'd cried and screamed that she wouldn't go unless they'd take Lucy too.

Lucy remembered the gazes of the people as they looked her over. Then they said that they didn't have enough food for more than one child. She knew they weren't telling the truth. They simply hadn't wanted her.

No one had.

She turned her face to the window, ignoring the useless tears clouding her vision.

She doubted any respectable man in the next town would want her. They'd probably see her scrawny frame and ugly face and turn away, disgusted. While she didn't want a husband, the thought of them turning their backs on her was too much to ponder.

Why did they have to have that stupid rule anyway?

In order to keep the orphan train from overflowing, the orphans were forced to leave when they reached the age of fifteen. If you were a boy, you were on your own to seek work. If you were a girl, you were given up to whatever man wanted you.

Well, not any man. They had to at least claim to be Christian.

Lucy tried to ignore the memory of Missie Lou, a girl that had been given away to a supposedly Christian man whose children had visible bruises on their faces, a testament of their father's cruelty. She shivered. *God, please give me a good man who truly follows You.*

She wanted a husband who was kind and generous and loved Jesus. She wondered if that was too much to ask for.

At least I'm not as young as others, she mused, attempting to change her mental subject. No matter what kind of husband she ended up with, it was better for her than others, seeing as she was seventeen.

She smiled in remembrance of her clever brother's trick. When she and her twin brother Travis first joined the orphan train, he instructed her to claim to be two years younger than she actually was. She had been young and small for her ten years and had easily passed as an eight-year-old. The hard part was what else Travis said. To pretend that they weren't related. She hadn't liked agreeing to that one but he said that they'd be less likely to be adopted if they were together.

Where was her brother now? She wished with all her heart that she had been able to obtain his address. He'd been taken from the orphan train when he was fourteen, adopted by an Indiana farmer who needed workers. She felt tears start again, remembering the day they were forced to say goodbye.

She'd been crying and knew Travis was struggling not to. He'd already packed his belongings and was about to leave. He held her close for as long as he could then pushed her back and kissed her wet cheek. He'd promised that when he could he'd come and find her one day, no matter where she was. She, in turn, had promised to pray for him every day.

She had yet to break that promise.

Where could Travis be? Did he still work for the same farmer? Was he out on his own? Did he have a job? Or a home? Did he live with a kind family, or a cruel one? Was he with someone?

She was surprised at that thought. She had never really thought of him actually getting hitched. It had never crossed her mind before now. But it was certainly possible. After all, she was soon to be wed herself.

No, she told herself sternly, *you are not going to go thinking about that again.*

She glanced down at the little girl who was closer than any friend. The stress of Lucy's imminent departure had tuckered Joan, who now slumbered against her breast. The child was more like a daughter to her. She'd practically raised her. And once her brother had left, Joan had received all her time and energy. Oh, she'd loved the other children too. But Joan was…well, Joan was hers.

She knew if they were separated, Joan wouldn't be the only one scarred. She wasn't sure if she could live without her little friend.

Please let me keep Joan, Lord. I know I'm asking a lot, but, please, if there's some way for us to stay together, make it happen.

She gazed out the window of the train car at the sinking sun. The ball of fire slowly slipped into the horizon, casting pink, purple, and orange hues across the clouds. The beauty and wonder in the display of God's handiwork helped to comfort Lucy. It seemed almost as if He was telling her that if He could take the sky and make something so beautiful of it every night, then how much more simple would it be for Him to answer her prayers? She just had to have faith.

She whispered a thank You to Him as she watched the sun disappear. What was that verse Mrs. Walton had had them memorize? "With God, all things are possible." Whatever happened to her, He would work His will. She clung to that promise as her eyes drifted shut.

Two

Lucy found herself wishing outlaws would come and stop the train. No, that wouldn't be good. They would steal everyone's belongings and, if they were wicked enough, possibly steal one of them too. No, that was a bad idea. What if something went wrong? Yes, something could cause one of the train parts to break down and the train would be unable to go forward and they would all have to walk back to the last town. That would work. Or perhaps they would ride right pass the next town and on to another one.

Apparently, trusting God didn't keep her from being nervous.

She combed her fingers through her hair in an attempt at taming it before separating it into three parts and weaving them together into a braid. She tied it with a worn ribbon, set it over her shoulder, then smoothed her dress.

She couldn't stop noticing how unappealing she

was. Old dress, frayed ribbon, ugly shoes, dirty hair, skinny frame, the list was endless. She let out a breath, shut her eyes, and warned her pessimistic mind to keep quiet. She attempted to swallow the lump in her throat and commanded herself not to cry.

God was in control. Whatever happened, she was in His hands.

Lucy clutched a small sack containing her few belongings as she waited for the train to stop. In just a matter of minutes, her fate would be decided.

She helped Mrs. Walton gather all the children, then to wash their faces and straighten their hair, so they would look their best. She had done it many times before, in every town they went through. They would stop at the local church and people interested in adopting would come, sign a paper, and take their child. Sometimes, nearly every child joined a new family and other times, only one or two children were taken. And with those that left the orphan train, others sometimes joined. Orphans from the town who had no one willing to care for them. Lucy hoped there were none from this town. She didn't want to live in a place where no one reached out a helping hand to those who needed it most.

Joan quickly claimed her hand as the train began to roll to a stop.

They pressed their faces to the window to see the town as it came into view. It was small and dusty. Shops lined both sides of the street and the church stood out of the town a bit, its spire standing tall in the sky. As the train continued forward, townsfolk could be seen standing along the boardwalk, some going about their business, others waiting for the train's arrival.

Lucy knew Mrs. Walton had wired ahead that the orphans were coming. She wondered how many of the people were waiting for them.

Be with us, Jesus.

The train finally came to a shuttering stop.

Mrs. Walton stood. "All right, children, do you all have your belongings? Quickly gather them and let's go. Follow me."

Lucy waited for the rest of the children to follow Mrs. Walton before joining. She and Joan brought up the rear of the line of children. Once the conductor opened the door, they all poured out onto the boardwalk.

She immediately felt eyes on her and scanned the crowd, searching for a glimpse of the man with whom she would join her life. There were several men watching the orphans but most of their gazes held pity and sadness. Only one man looked upon her with interest and she shivered at how he scandalously eyed her up and down.

Please don't let him be the one, God. Please.

"Come along, children."

Lucy turned back to her fellow orphans as Mrs. Walton continued on toward the church building. She helped herd the children after her, Joan clinging tightly to her hand.

A man of the cloth stepped out of the church as they approached and Mrs. Walton greeted the minister. "Parson Rector, I have brought the children. I assume all is in order for us to begin right away?"

"Yes, Mrs. Walton, we are ready. I pray the citizens of this town will open their hearts to these dear children." He smiled at the orphans and Lucy felt her heart warm at his kindness.

"As do I. Thank you for allowing us to use your building. May we proceed?"

"Yes, of course." The pastor led them into the church. "And we are thankful that you have allowed us to be a part of your ministry. You may assemble the children up here on the platform and I'll go ring the bell." He hurried to the entrance and disappeared outside.

"Come, children. You all stand up here oldest to youngest," Mrs. Walton instructed.

Lucy looked to Joan, who still clutched her hand. "Go ahead, Joan."

Her eyes began filling. "But I want to stand with you."

"You may stand with Lucy, Joan," Mrs. Walton interjected. "But once either of you get a home of your own, you'll have to say goodbye. Understand?"

The little girl nodded.

Lucy stepped up onto the platform at the end of the line of children. She crouched down to look Joan in the eye. "Remember, Joan, you want to get adopted this time because then you and I can be in the same town.

And if you aren't, I'll make sure to ask the man who I marry to adopt you, okay? So you can't fight them if someone wants to keep you. If you do, we might never see each other again."

Joan nodded, her eyes watery. "I want to stay with you."

Lucy pulled her close. "I'll do my best to keep us together."

She wouldn't tell her that if she ended up with the man who was watching her before, she would never mention her little friend. A life apart from Lucy was better than abuse.

The parson reentered the building to tell them of the approaching townspeople and Lucy rubbed away Joan's tears and quickly straightened.

It was time.

Townsfolk entered the building one by one, men, women, and children. Some gazed at the orphans keenly, taking all aspects into consideration. Others were obviously there solely out of curiosity, with no interest in adopting. There were over a dozen people when the flow ceased. They all took their seats and talked quietly amongst themselves before the pastor stepped up.

"Hello, everyone. Today we have some visitors from the orphan train. Mrs. Walton is here in care of the children and will tell you all you need to know about them. Please take these children into consideration this afternoon. Each child needs a home, needs loved ones to care for them and provide for their physical, emotional, and spiritual needs. Let God work in your heart concerning these dear souls. Mrs. Walton."

The woman stepped forward. "Thank you, Parson. I will tell you some about each child. Please raise your hand if you would like to adopt and I have a paper here for you to sign, with the parson as witness.

"First, is little Charlie Reynolds…"

Lucy lost track of Mrs. Walton's words as she continued.

The man was there. He sat near the back of the building and stared at her openly, his eyes trailing her body from her head to her feet. She kept her gaze lowered and fought the fear that rose in her throat. *Please let there be someone else, God. Please.*

Her head came up swiftly when she heard Joan's name mentioned. There were only a few people left in the pews and it appeared as though three children had been adopted. Six of them were left.

Joan squeezed Lucy's hand and gave her a desperate look before stepping forward.

No one spoke up. No one was willing to adopt her.

Tears sprang to Lucy's eyes as Joan returned to her side. This was probably the last time she would ever see her. Lucy would most likely be forced to marry the wicked man and she would see the last of her little friend. At least if someone else adopted her, they would see each other at church and shindigs, but if Joan didn't stay in the same town, it was unlikely they would ever see each other again.

"And this is Lucille Weber. She joined our orphan train at the age of eight and is now fifteen years old. She is of good health and does well with children. She would make an excellent wife and mother."

Lucy released Joan's little hand and stepped forward.

"I'll take her."

She knew who had spoken before she looked up. The man met her gaze with a lustful gleam in his eyes.

"Where's the paper claimin' her? I'll sign it right now. Been needin' me a good woman."

Lucy shivered.

Parson Rector hesitated.

"What is it, Parson? Don't think I'll take care of her? I'll be good to her. And soon as this lady here is done, I'll need you to perform us a marriage ceremony."

"Clem, I'm not sure I feel right signing this girl over to you."

"Whyever not, Parson? Me and her are gonna be best friends, ain't that right, girl?"

Lucy froze, fear licking at her consciousness.

"Speak up, girl!"

She stared wide-eyed at the man's angry face. He reached up and took a hold of her arm, pulling her off the platform. Lucy let out a cry, tripping at the momentum and landing hard on her knees.

"Lucy!" Joan cried, rushing for her.

"Stay away from her, little girl! She's just fine, pretending to fall. Get up."

Lucy scrambled to her feet. She would punch him if

15

he dared to lay a hand on Joan. She looked down at her. "I-I'm fine, Joan."

"Well, Parson, you gonna sign it?"

"I—"

"Look, Parson, there ain't no one else that wants this girl. I'm being a Christian here, by offering to help. If I don't take her, she'll go back with them orphans. You said they needed a home and that's what I'm providin'. Now, you gonna sign that paper or not?"

Indecision warred in the pastor's eyes. "Is there anyone present willing to take this young woman?"

No one spoke up.

Clem laughed. "See? I told you, Parson. I'm the only one here that wants her. Me and this missy are gonna get along just fine." He wrapped an arm around Lucy's waist and she pulled away. He yanked her against him and she gasped.

"Take your hands off her, Clem Toeger."

They all turned to see who had spoken.

A man stood in the center of the church aisle. He stood as though ready for a fight, feet spread apart, hands clenched into tight fists at his sides. His eyes narrowed as he took in Clem's rough treatment of Lucy.

"What do you want, Black? Need a woman to warm your bed? You can't have this one. She's mine." Clem sneered.

Lucy shut her eyes in horror. *I beg You, Lord Jesus. Please do not let me belong to this wretched man.*

"I said, take your hands off her." The man's voice was lethal and Clem reluctantly released his hold.

The parson spoke up. "Garrett, Clem is the only one willing to take this young woman here. Unless you're willing to take her in, I'll have to sign her over to him. What do you say?"

Lucy felt the man's eyes on her and looked up. His face held kindness, curiosity, and sympathy. She silently pleaded with him to do something. She would much rather marry him than Clem.

"What's your name?" he asked.

"L-Lucy Weber. W-What's yours?"

"Garrett Black. Would you rather be joined to Clem here, miss, or me?"

Clem sputtered. "You're asking the girl what she wants? Who cares?"

"I do, Clem. Shut your trap and let her speak." He turned back to her.

Lucy's gaze never wavered from his face. "You."

Garrett smiled.

"It ain't up to her, Black! I was here first and I claimed her! She's mine!" Clem's face tightened in anger.

"You don't have any claim on her, Clem." The parson signed the paper and handed it to Garrett, who did the same. "She belongs to Garrett, free and clear."

"I'll get you for this, Black!" Clem seethed before turning and storming out of the church.

Lucy released a breath when he was out of sight. A

familiar hand slipped into hers and she knelt and gave Joan a hug. Tears of relief misted.

Mrs. Walton's voice sounded. "Well, that's all for today, children. Let's go find a place to stay for the night. Come, Joan."

Joan's head shot up and she looked at Lucy. "I want to stay with you."

Lucy nodded and swiped at her cheeks. "Let me ask Mr. Black, okay?"

Mrs. Walton came and grasped Joan's hand. "Come along, Joan."

"No! I'm staying with Lucy!" she shrieked in panic, tears immediately forming.

Lucy turned to her new guardian. "Can you please adopt her, Mr. Black? Sh-she's like a daughter to me. I can't imagine living without her. Please? I-I'll do whatever you want. I—"

He touched a finger to her mouth to quiet her. "We can adopt her."

Joy flooded her soul. "Thank you! Thank you so much!" She quickly told Mrs. Walton what he had said and she handed him a paper to sign. Joan launched herself at Lucy and she lifted the little girl into her arms.

"I can stay with you, Lucy! I can stay with you!" She beamed, looking happier than Lucy had ever seen her before.

"Yes, Joan, you can stay with me." Lucy smiled, battling her tears. She looked up at Mr. Black. "Thank you so much. I don't know how I can show you how grateful I am."

His mouth tugged upward in a smile. "Don't mention it."

"Garrett, do I have a wedding ceremony to perform?" the parson asked.

Garrett looked at her. "Would you like to eat first? Or is there anything you need to do?"

Lucy shook her head, her grin faltering. She wanted to get this over with as soon as possible. "N-now is fine, I suppose."

His green eyes suddenly became dark and unreadable as he returned his focus to the man of the cloth. "Parson?"

The preacher smiled. "Dearly beloved, we are gathered here today…"

Lucy watched her soon-to-be husband as the parson went on. She prayed he was all he seemed to be. If he had adopted her, she'd have to stay with him until she was an adult. But with marrying him, their lives were joined forever. She would live with him for the rest of her life.

She realized that she knew nothing about him. A million questions swarmed in her mind. How old was he? What did he do for a living? Did he have brothers and sisters? Had he ever been married? Were his parents alive? Did he get his looks from his father or mother?

She blushed at the thought. He was a good-looking man. His shirt was strained slightly across his chest and shoulders, the muscles showing beneath evidencing that he worked hard. His brown hair was wavy, soft, and inviting. His face had a bit of a stern set to it, but his green eyes and stubble lessened the hardness. His mouth was—

"Lucy?"

Flames licked up her face as she realized he caught her staring. She cleared her throat. "Y-yes?"

Garrett tipped his head toward the parson and Lucy turned to him, refocusing her attention.

"Do you, Lucille Weber, take Garrett Black to be your lawfully wedded husband?"

Lucy swallowed hard and nodded, not looking at Garrett. "I-I do."

"Do you, Garrett Black, take Lucille Weber to be your lawfully wedded wife?"

"I do."

Lucy felt Garrett's eyes on her but she kept her attention on the parson.

"What God hath joined together, let no man put asunder. Garrett, you may kiss the bride."

She had forgotten about that part. Would he really kiss her? She wasn't sure whether she wanted him to or not. Lucy turned to her husband, who was gazing at her intently. He leaned down and gently bussed her cheek. Heat warmed her cheeks and she looked away as he pulled back.

Someone tugged at her hand and she glanced down. Joan. How could she have forgotten about her?

"Does that mean you're my mama now, Lucy?"

She paused. Was she? "I-I think it does, Joan."

"I like that." The little girl smiled.

Garrett crouched down before Joan. "Hello. My name's Garrett."

Joan launched herself into his arms. His confused gaze met Lucy's and she grinned. Joan pulled back. "I'm Joan. Thank you for 'dopting me. I want to stay with Lucy."

"I'll make sure that you do, Joan." Garrett straightened. "Now, would you two ladies like to come with me down to the diner and have a late supper?"

Joan nodded adamantly.

"Yes, Mr. Black, we'd love to."

"Call me Garrett, Lucy."

She nodded. "We'd love to, Garrett."

Three

Garrett couldn't believe what he had done.

He had driven into town to purchase supplies. Never in his life had he considered that he'd return that night with two females in his company.

One being his wife and the other his daughter.

He glanced to his side where Lucy held Joan in her lap. They had both fallen asleep during the four-hour drive back to his ranch. Lucy's head rested gently against his shoulder, her hair beginning to come loose from its braid. His wife.

He was married.

What would his family say? His ma would be shocked. She'd probably cry and welcome Lucy with open arms. His pa would be proud of him for rescuing her and advise him on how to be a good husband. His sisters would be exuberant and shower her with gifts. His brothers would tease and pledge to protect their new sister-in-law.

What happened to Lucy's family? She was an orphan, that much he had gathered. Did she have any siblings? Any aunts or uncles? What caused her to join the orphan train? He had many unanswered questions and would probably have to wait until tomorrow to hear the answers.

Garrett wished he'd known earlier that he was getting married. That way he could have prepared. Where would she sleep? He would have to make up the guest room for Lucy and Joan to share. He seriously doubted either he or Lucy were prepared to share his bedroom. Heat thrummed through his body and he let out a fast breath. Definitely not ready.

As the wagon reached his barn, Miguel, his foreman, approached, his gaze curious as he took in the sight of Lucy and Joan.

"I'll explain later."

Miguel nodded wordlessly.

Garrett turned to his bride. He shook her gently. "Lucy. Lucy."

Her eyes opened slowly, a haze of sleep clouding them for a moment. She sat up and yawned. "How long was I asleep?"

"About an hour. We're at my ranch."

"Mm," she murmured distractedly and glanced around.

"I'll take Joan." Garrett reached for the little girl and Lucy reluctantly placed her in his outstretched arms. He climbed down off the buckboard and she followed suit.

They walked to his house and Garrett opened the door and motioned her inside. Or wasn't he supposed to carry her over the threshold? It would be a little difficult while holding Joan though. He decided to skip that rule.

He led Lucy to his guest bedroom and slowly lowered Joan, who was still sleeping, onto the bed. He turned to his wife to find her staring at him. "I'll leave you to do whatever you need."

She nodded and he left the room, releasing a breath. He wasn't sure if he'd get any sleep tonight.

What did he mean by that?

"I'll leave you to do whatever you need."

Was he wanting her to stay with Joan? Or was he wanting her to put Joan in bed and then follow him?

Lucy swallowed hard.

She didn't know much about what went on between a married couple, but she didn't want to explore it with a complete stranger. Was that what he was expecting?

She tried to ignore the thought and walked to the side of the bed where Garrett had placed Joan. She pulled the covers down beneath her little friend and then laid them over her. She dropped a kiss on Joan's forehead. "Good night," she whispered.

Lucy turned and found a hand mirror sitting on a dresser. She picked it up and studied herself, the moonlight streaming through a window lending her light. She looked tired and more than a bit scared. She set it back down.

Was Garrett expecting her to join him? Her stomach clenched at the thought. Was he really the kind man that he seemed to be? She prayed so. But either way, she figured she had to go see him. If he was waiting for her and she didn't come, he might become angry. And anger often caused people to strike out at those around them. She couldn't risk that.

She took a deep breath and prayed he had gone to sleep before opening the door.

Garrett knew he wouldn't be able to fall asleep, so he sat in the sitting room and watched the lantern he had lit as it burned.

He turned when he heard the door to the guest room open.

Lucy approached him slowly, trepidation marking her forehead.

"What is it?"

She opened her mouth. "I…" She paused, was silent for a moment, and then began again, her eyes on the floor. "I don't know much about w-wife things."

What was that supposed to mean? She didn't know how to cook? Why was she telling him this now?

She peeked up at him and must have seen his confusion. "I mean, about…other things." She sucked in a breath. "But, if-if you want to. I mean, I-I'm your wife and you probably are thinking that we…"

Understanding dawned. Garrett reached for her hand and grasped it. The poor girl. She was trembling.

He dipped his head and met her gaze. "I would rather we wait for a while, until we're both comfortable. I think we have plenty time for that later."

She nodded, some of the tension draining from her shoulders.

"Would you like to sit down?"

She nodded again and took a seat, watching him expectantly.

Garrett smiled. "Do you have any questions for me? We hardly know each other."

"How old are you?"

"I'm twenty-four. And you're fifteen?" He tried not to wince. That would make him nearly ten years her senior.

"No. I'm actually seventeen."

"You are? I thought the other lady—"

"Mrs. Walton doesn't know. She thinks I'm fifteen." Lucy smiled. "She was tricked."

His brow furrowed. He wasn't so sure it was good that his new wife was pleased about deceiving someone.

"It was my brother's idea," she explained.

"You have a brother?"

Lucy nodded. "Travis. He's my twin. We joined the train when we were both ten, but he told me to say I was eight instead. He knew that people are more likely to adopt younger children."

"Where is Travis now?"

Her eyes misted. "I don't know. He left the orphan train when we were fourteen. Was adopted by a farmer in Indiana who needed help with his crops. I haven't heard from him since."

He frowned. She'd been all alone after that? "I'm sorry."

"Me too." She wiped away a tear. "Do you have any brothers or sisters?"

"I do. Two older brothers and three younger sisters."

"What are their names?"

"Well, there is William. He's twenty-eight and is married with four children. His wife's name is Heidi and their children are Hans, Rebekah, Lucas, and Anne.

"Then there's Richard. He is twenty-six, also married, and has three children. His wife is Miriam and their children's names are Jacob, Joshua, and Lydia.

"After me is Courtney. She is twenty-two and just married her husband Sean a few months ago.

"Next is April. She's twenty and has a slew of men at her disposal, though she would rather read than socialize.

"Lastly, there's Ellen. She's eighteen and has a very bright personality. She speaks her mind, which sometimes lands her in trouble, and she loves to laugh.

"And my parents are Thomas and Sarah. They have been married for almost thirty years and do pretty much everything together."

Lucy smiled. "Your family sounds wonderful. I would like to meet them."

"I know they would want to meet you too."

"They would?" A wrinkle furrowed between her brows.

Garrett frowned. "Why are you surprised? Of course they would. You're my wife."

She shrugged. "Not everyone takes kindly to orphans."

Had she faced ridicule because of her lack of family? The thought saddened him. "My family never has been and never will be those kind of people. We believe all people are equal, no matter their race or their background."

Silence stretched between them for a moment before he spoke again. "Do you have any other brothers or sisters?"

She shook her head. "No. My mother had more children after Travis and me, but they all died. One time she died too. After that, my father wasn't the same. He would go off, sometimes for weeks, and wander the woods. And then one day he was out during a storm. He was swept into a river and drowned."

He couldn't imagine a child having to face such loss. "Did you not have any friends or family to take you in?"

She shook her head. "Our parents moved here from France. We had no way to contact any relatives and even if we did, we didn't know who they were. We didn't know many people and those we did, couldn't or wouldn't help us. So we joined the orphan train."

Garrett wondered just what all his wife had gone

through in her seventeen years.

Lucy yawned and he smiled at the innocence in her face. "We should probably go to sleep."

She nodded and they stood.

"You and Joan can share that room. Mine is right there if you ever need to get me." He gestured to it.

"Okay." She started for her room.

"Lucy?"

She turned around. "Yes?"

"Do you believe in God?"

"Yes, of course."

"Would you mind if I prayed?"

She shook her head, her eyes brightening. "Not at all. I would like that."

He smiled and then bowed his head. "Dear God, thank You for all You have done for us today. Thank You for bringing Lucy and Joan into my life, Lord. Please bless us and help us to dwell together in unity. Give us the rest we need tonight and help us to count our blessings. We praise You, Jesus, and thank You for all You've given us. Amen."

Garrett opened his eyes, leaned down, and pressed a gentle kiss to Lucy's cheek. "Sweet dreams."

Four

"Lucy! Lucy, wake up!"

Lucy reluctantly opened her eyes to see Joan yanking the covers off of her. It took a moment before everything came back. *I'm married.*

"Mr. Garrett made us some sausage and eggs. He's waitin' in the kitchen. I already ate 'cuz I didn't want to wait and they were real yummy. Lots better than the porridge Mrs. Walton gave us."

A grin tugged at Lucy's mouth. She couldn't recall seeing Joan so chattery. It appeared as though she fully accepted this place as her home. It warmed her heart to see her so happy.

"Are you coming? It's been ready for an awful long time and Mr. Garrett, he already had his coffee and I asked him for a drink and he let me have one. It's nasty! I can't know why he likes it. He says some people put cream and sugar in it but he don't like it that way, so he drinks it plain. And he's still waitin' for you and he's got your breakfast. Are you coming, Lucy? Are you coming?"

"Yes, Joan, I'm coming, I'm coming." Lucy laughed at her exuberance.

She quickly made the bed and straightened her appearance before letting Joan lead her out of their bedroom. The little girl pulled her into the kitchen where Garrett was seated at a simple table with four chairs. His gaze rested on hers and a shy smile built on her face as she remembered his chaste kiss from the night before. "Good morning."

He stood and motioned for her to sit next to him. "Good morning. Did you sleep well?"

She took a seat and waited to speak until he followed suit. "I did, thank you."

He nodded and motioned to the plate before her. "It's not much, but it's kept me fed the past couple of years."

"I'm sure it's fine."

Lucy bowed her head to pray. *Dear God, bless this food. Thank You for giving Joan and me a good home. Please keep us safe and bless Garrett for taking us in. Help everything to work out and please, if You could, let Garrett come to love me and teach me to love him. Amen.*

She quickly took a bite of her scrambled eggs and chewed.

"Do you like it?"

Lucy nodded. "Yes, it's very good."

He smiled.

"I like it!" Joan piped up. "Even better than the sausage."

Lucy ate some of the meat and her taste buds sighed in appreciation of the flavors. "Mmm... That's the best sausage I've ever had. I would like it if you could teach me how to make it."

"Do you know how to cook?"

"Not very much. I cooked for me and Travis and my father after my mother died, but I haven't had much of an opportunity to since then, I'm afraid. We ate mostly sandwiches on the orphan train."

"I would be willing to teach you when we have time. I usually work around the ranch with my cowhands during the day but I can teach you something new for supper each night."

"I'd like that." Lucy continued to enjoy her meal, feeling self-conscious as Garrett and Joan watched her. "Do you need to work today?"

He shook his head. "No. I decided to show you two around today."

"Oh."

"How many people do you have workin' for you, Mr. Garrett?" Joan asked with wide eyes. "I bet it's lots."

Garrett chuckled. "I have eleven cowhands, along with my foreman, Miguel. I have already told them about the both of you and instructed them to treat you with the same respect they would me."

"Thank you." Lucy smiled at her husband.

He shrugged. "There's nothing to thank me for.

You and Joan are part of my family and I expect you to be treated as such."

Her heart warmed. She had a feeling their marriage would get along just fine.

Once she was finished with her breakfast, Garrett led her and Joan outside.

"First is the stable, with all of our horses."

"Look, Joan, look at this one! Isn't she pretty?"

"That's Autumn. She's a sweet tempered horse, and is very good around children." Garrett lifted Joan up so she could pet the horse.

They continued through the stable, Lucy and Joan exclaiming over each one as Garrett explained and answered their questions.

"They are all so beautiful!" Lucy gushed.

"Do you know how to ride?" Garrett asked with a bright grin.

She shook her head. "I rode a little bit when I was young, but I don't really remember."

"I'll have to teach you how."

Apprehension filled her. "Oh, I don't know. Horses are pretty big. They-they could throw me and crush me without even thinking about it."

"Are you afraid of horses?" Surprise rang in his voice. After she'd oohed and ahhed over them a minute ago, he'd probably thought she loved the animals. Which she did. Just in a different way.

She nodded slightly. "I like them a lot, b-but they're so big and strong."

"Don't worry. You'll overcome your fear after you learn to ride."

She nodded again, though she couldn't help but doubt his words a bit.

"I want to ride one!" Joan interjected.

"Well, then, I'll have to teach you too." Garrett smiled at the little one in his arms.

Garrett showed them some of his stock of cattle – three thousand bovine. Lucy couldn't remember ever seeing so many cows. He said they let them graze and wander and, when the time came, they drove part of the herd into the city and sold them. They made a profit with each delivery.

Garrett introduced her and Joan to Miguel, his foreman. She had a feeling the Mexican cowboy was a firm, no-nonsense person as a sharp tip of his hat was all he'd given by way of greeting before returning to his work. She also met three of the ranch hands – Billy, Louis, and Sam. Billy was a talkative, reckless boy no older than she was. Louis was a light-skinned black man and offered to teach her French when she told him she didn't remember how to speak it. Sam was a kind cowpoke in his fifties who was doing his best to keep the rest of them out of trouble.

Afterwards, Garrett took her to a spot where she could see for miles. He showed her the vastness of his land. Over a thousand acres of pure Texas country. She could hardly believe this was her home now. Her husband said he planned for them to ride out together so he could show her some of the land once she was comfortable riding a horse.

Garrett led her and Joan to the chicken coop, where the squawking flock provided eggs and the occasional roast. Lucy offered to feed them each day and he gave her instructions.

The garden was to the left of the house. It grew a small abundance of lettuce, cabbage, broccoli, cauliflower, carrots, eggplant, garlic, parsley, pepper, potatoes, spinach, squash, tomatoes, and watermelon.

They lived about forty miles from town, Garrett informed her. He usually made the trip to Saddle once a month for supplies. With meat and milk from the cows, eggs from the chickens, and the vegetable garden, there wasn't much they needed in town.

Their nearest neighbors, the Johnstons, were six miles away. Garrett was best friends with the family and planned to take her and Joan to visit them soon. Lucy learned that one of their daughters was near her age.

On Sundays, church was held at nine o'clock at Mack Walters' homestead. The rancher decided to start his own little church for the people too far from town to drive there for worship every week. Sometimes other ranchers or ranch hands preached, but it was mostly Mack Walters.

Sunday was the only event day in the week. The rest were ordinary, just taking care of the ranch and living.

The sun began dipping toward the horizon when Garrett led Lucy and Joan inside.

"Today, we'll have cabbage, potatoes, and beef mash for supper," Garrett said, depositing a cabbage and four potatoes he'd taken from the garden into the sink.

"What's that?" Joan asked.

"It's cabbage and potatoes and beef cooked up and mixed together."

"Oh." The little girl smiled widely.

Lucy spoke up. "How do you want me to help?"

"After I clean these off, I'll let you chop them up while I get water for the cabbage." He swiftly rinsed the vegetables and demonstrated what size they should be cut before pumping water into a pot and setting it on the wood stove. "When the cabbage is chopped, we'll put it in the pot to boil. Then we'll fry up the potatoes and the beef."

Lucy continued cutting the cabbage as Garrett started on the meat. Once she was finished, she dropped the vegetable into the pot of hot water and started on the potatoes. "Do you put any seasonings into it?"

Garret nodded. "Salt, pepper and oil with the potatoes and meat and butter with the cabbage. Sometimes I have it with bread too but I'm out of bread right now. Maybe tomorrow I can teach you how to bake some bread."

Lucy smiled. "I love fresh bread."

"Lucy!" Joan whined. "I'm hungry."

"It's not ready yet, Joan. You'll have to wait a while longer."

"But I'm bored!"

"Well, then, you'll have to find something to do to keep yourself busy."

Garrett left the kitchen then returned from his bedroom a moment later. He held out wooden figurines to Joan. "Here. My pa gave these to me when I wasn't much older than you. You can keep them if you'd like, but you have to take real good care of them."

"I will!" Joan snatched them from his hands, a smile widening her face.

"What do you say, Joan?" Lucy reminded.

"Thank you, Mr. Garrett!" Joan promptly marched to the sitting room as she introduced the wooden people to each other in different voices.

"Thank you for giving those to her. That was kind of you."

Garrett grinned. "I remember when my pa gave them to me. Was the best thing ever. Don't use them much anymore."

"I had a doll that I loved when I was young. My mother made it for me when I was a baby."

"What happened to it?"

She sighed. "I don't know. It disappeared one day when I was on the orphan train. I suspect one of the other girls took it. But whoever did probably needed it more than I did. I had Travis."

Garrett remained silent, stirring the potatoes and beef back and forth in their pan. "What was it like? Living on the orphan train?"

She shrugged. "It was a passel of children and Mrs. Walton. We all lived together, like a big family. Girls and boys separate, of course. We traveled mostly. Stopped at towns. I was a caretaker of the children, in a way. I liked to help Mrs. Walton with them. To train them to behave their best, to cheer them. They…we were always nervous when it came to being presented for the town. Some were adopted… And some weren't."

Garrett taste-tested the cabbage and found it had cooked all the way through. He drained the hot water from the pot before showing Lucy how much butter to mix into it, and then he dumped it into the pan of nearly-done beef and potatoes.

"I imagine it was difficult, not being adopted."

Lucy looked away. She didn't want Garrett to decide he didn't want her either. She longed to be with someone who actually wanted her – and not for what she could give to them. If he began to wonder why no one else had accepted her, he would turn against her himself. She couldn't live with that. Not when she'd already begun to hope he could one day love her.

A hand suddenly warmed her shoulder. She whirled around.

Garrett's eyes were shadowed with questions. "You can talk to me about it if you want."

She shook her head, doing her best to dismiss his concerns. "I should probably go get Joan. It looks as though supper is ready." She hurried from the kitchen, releasing a breath she just realized she'd been holding.

Oh, God, please don't let this end. I know I can love Garrett, Lord. Please don't let him reject me too.

After clearing her thoughts for a moment, she found

Joan in the sitting room. The little girl was still playing with the wooden toys and Lucy paused for a moment to listen.

"'You can't get me!'" One figurine declared to the other, Joan bouncing them to indicate who was speaking. "'Yes, I can!' 'No, you can't!' 'Yes, I can! Watch me!'" The one charged the other and they raced around the empty fireplace.

"Joan."

The little girl looked up. "Yes?"

"Supper's ready. Do you want to help set the table?"

"Set the table!" She jumped up and rushed to the kitchen ahead of Lucy.

Garrett handed Joan the plates and utensils before meeting Lucy's gaze. She looked away, escaping his probing look by taking Joan to the table and showing her where each setting belonged.

He soon brought the meal to the table and they all sat and bowed their heads as Garrett blessed the food.

After echoing the "amen," Lucy dug into her food. "Mmm, this is delicious, Garrett. I like it."

He smiled. "It's something my ma invented. The other boys didn't like it much, but I did."

She nodded.

"I like it too!" Joan added, half of her clumsy bites falling from her fork onto the table only to be lifted to her mouth with her fingers.

"Joan, use your fork. And bring your plate closer to you so you don't spill."

The little girl followed her instructions and successfully got a bite to her mouth in one piece, grinning at her as she chewed.

A smile stretched Lucy's mouth at the innocent serenity in Joan's expression. So sweet. At moments like this, she was extremely grateful that Joan had joined the orphan train so young and didn't remember her past. Whatever it was would probably never allow that look of joy to cross the little girl's face.

Lucy felt eyes on her and glanced up to find Garrett looking at her questioningly. She blinked, suddenly realizing the moisture in her eyes, and turned back to her food as she lectured her mind to give her a break.

"I would like to visit my family soon, if you wouldn't mind," Garrett spoke up. "They live on the other side of Saddle, about seven hours from here by wagon. It's a long drive, but I haven't seen them in a while. And everyone will want to meet the new additions to the family."

Warmth brushed her face as Lucy wondered what his family would think of her and Joan. Immediate hesitation registered but she did her best to push it from her mind. From what Garrett had said the night before, they were all wonderful. And wouldn't she like to visit her new in-laws?

"What do you think about that, Joan?" Lucy asked. "Would you like to meet Mr. Garrett's ma and pa and brothers and sisters?"

"Yes!" Joan beamed.

"Well then." Lucy looked back at her husband. "We're all in agreement."

"Good." Pleasure lit his countenance.

"When are you wanting to go?"

"I was thinking probably on Monday, two days from now. My parents will want us to stay for a while and we can head back on Saturday."

"That sounds like a good plan."

Garrett grinned. "Monday it is, then."

Five

A smile clung to Garrett's lips. The previous night ran through his head. He and Lucy didn't get a chance to talk as they had the night before since Sunday began early. But when the time came to say good night and he pressed a kiss to her cheek, she slowly pushed him away from her with a hand against his chest. Her "good night, Garrett" was soft, yet rushed and she quickly left him for the sanctuary of her bedroom. The entire scene would have left him discouraged if he hadn't noticed how she met his gaze for a second before leaving. The emotion swirling in her eyes told him that his attraction to her wasn't one-sided.

He'd been grinning like a fool ever since.

Usually, he and some of his ranch hands rode out to Mack Walters' spread. But today they'd have to hitch up the buckboard with Lucy and Joan along, which was why he was outside, not to mention that the girls needed privacy as they bathed.

Garrett grabbed the correct harness and began placing it on the waiting horse. He wondered about Lucy's hesitance the night before. Why had she become so quiet when he asked about not being adopted and then avoided him after that? And why were there tears in her eyes as she watched Joan while they ate? The questions racing through his mind reminded him that he didn't know his wife as well as he wished. But he planned to remedy that – and fast.

Once he was finished, he headed for the house. He needed to change into his Sunday clothes before they got going. He paused before opening the door and, feeling foolish, knocked.

The door opened and Joan grinned up at him. "Why are you knocking at your own house, Mr. Garrett?"

"Well, I didn't want to catch you ladies unawares."

"What's un-wares mean?"

"I didn't want to surprise you while you were getting ready."

"Oh, you didn't. We're ready and Lucy's fixin' her hair. She already did mine, see?" The little girl tilted her head in his direction to show her pigtail braids.

"I see. They're very pretty. Would you mind if I come in so I can get dressed for church?"

"Oh! 'Course, Mr. Garrett." She stepped aside and let him pass.

He hurried to his room and readied himself for church. He was finished in a few moments and exited his bedroom to find Lucy and Joan waiting for him. He noticed that their clothes, though different from the dresses they wore the previous days, were a bit faded and made a mental note to take Lucy to the mercantile and purchase some material for her. Unless she didn't know how to sew? He'd have to ask her. Maybe his mother could teach her how to sew if she couldn't.

His eyes roamed to his wife's hair. It was twisted and pinned up behind her head in a simple yet elegant bun and small, blonde wisps already escaped their confines and rested gently against her slender neck.

He quickly refocused his attention. "Are you ready to go?"

Lucy's mouth tilted upward in a small smile. "We are."

Garrett escorted his girls out to the wagon and helped them into it. In no time at all, they were on their way to Walters' with some of the ranch hands bringing up the rear.

The ride to Mack Walters' spread took a little more than an hour. Lucy's hands fiddled aimlessly with the front of her dress as they pulled up to the barn. He grasped her hand and gave it a squeeze. Her eyes widened in surprise. "Don't be nervous. I'm here with you." He gave her a smile and she hesitantly returned it. He tethered the horse to a hitching post and helped Lucy down from the buckboard, wishing he could hold her trim waist in his hands longer.

Garrett led his new wife and daughter up to Mack's house.

Mack Walters greeted them at the door. "Morning, Garrett. Who's that you have with you?"

"Mack, this is my wife, Lucy, and my daughter, Joan."

His eyebrows rose. "Nice to meet you, Mrs. Black, and you too, little missy."

Joan piped up, "My name's not little missy. It's Joan."

"Well, I'm sorry, Joan. I didn't mean to call you something you're not." Mack grinned at the little girl.

"That's okay. I'll forgive you." The skin around Joan's eyes crinkled in delight.

Mack chuckled. "Well, thank you." He turned to Garrett. "You may go on inside. Ford Allen and the Palmers are already here."

"Thanks, Mack."

Garrett ushered Lucy and Joan inside the house and introduced them to their new neighbors. They entered the sitting room, which was converted into a miniature church house with enough seats for thirty people. Since Mack lived alone, he had more space than he needed and was easily able to make room for a small congregation. They took a seat and waited as more friends arrived and met Lucy and Joan. Garrett's heart swelled with pride as he introduced Lucy as "my wife." The Johnstons entered just a moment before services began so he was unable to let them meet Lucy until later.

The service began with a prayer, and then they sang a couple songs. Mack then stood up and brought them their weekly message, about God's blessings on their lives. He contrasted the circumstances of the Israelites from slavery in Egypt to their wandering in the wilderness, and how they continued to groan and complain even when God continually answered their prayers. He challenged them to always be grateful for their circumstances and to continually count their blessings. He finished his sermon with a prayer and they all sang another hymn before dismissing.

Garrett whispered in Lucy's ear, "I want you to meet the Johnstons." He guided her toward the family, her back warm against his palm. "Peter, Rose, this is my wife, Lucy."

Rose's eyes widened. "Wife? Why, land sakes, Garrett, when'd this come about?"

"Just last Friday." He grinned.

"Goodness gracious, you sure don't give any warning." She turned to Lucy. "You mean this beautiful young woman is your wife?"

Garrett nodded. "Sure is."

"Now, I don't think I've ever seen you before. Do you live in Saddle?"

He wondered if he should answer for Lucy or leave her to it.

"No, ma'am. I-I came here on the orphan train."

"Well, what do you know about that? It's nice to meet you, Lucy." Rose wrapped her in a hug and sneakily pulled her away from Garrett and Peter, leaving them to talk.

"How in the world did you end up hitched, Garrett? Thought you were tellin' me just a couple weeks ago that you weren't lonely for a wife." Peter eyed him, his eyebrow arched over its usual spot.

"I didn't plan on getting married. It just happened."

"How?"

Garrett briefly explained the situation.

"So it's just a marriage of convenience?"

He nodded.

"Are you satisfied with that?"

Garrett shrugged. "Don't plan on living like that for long."

"So you're not…sharing a bedroom?"

Garrett shook his head, heat crawling up his neck. "No, of course not. We're not ready for that. We don't even know each other yet."

"Ah. But you've thought on it some." Peter grinned knowingly.

The heat intensified. "Some," he admitted grudgingly.

"Have you talked about it at all?"

"Just to agree not to."

"And have you shared anything else? You know, kissed her or anything?"

This conversation was turning more uncomfortable by the minute. "Why do you want to know?"

Peter chuckled. "I'm just asking. Rose is gonna pepper me with questions later and if I don't have sufficient answers, she'll come after you too."

"I'll just say I'm working on it."

"On what?"

"On establishing a proper husband and wife relationship."

"Well, don't take it too fast. If you do that, you'll scare her. That's one thing I learned: Never pressure a woman before her time. You won't appreciate the results."

Garrett nodded. "I'll try to be patient."

"Good." Peter gestured toward where Lucy and Rose stood talking. "Shall we rejoin our wives?"

Garrett smiled. "Sounds like a great idea."

Lucy didn't protest as Rose led her away from Garrett and Mr. Johnston. She already knew she liked this woman and had a feeling they'd become fast friends.

"I'm Rose Johnston. That there, talking to your husband, is my husband, Peter, and running around here somewhere are our children. We've got seven of them. Marie, Daniel, Stephen, Gabriel, Andrew, Hope, and Jonas, though Marie's home now. Wasn't feeling well." Rose paused and turned to smile at Joan. "And who is this you have with you?"

"This is Joan. She rode the orphan train as well."

"Well, hello there, Joan. I got a daughter around here that's about your age. I'm sure she'd love the company if you wanted to go play with her."

Joan nodded enthusiastically and went off to find Hope

Rose turned back to Lucy. "You know, school's too far for any of us homesteaders out here to have our children attend, so I school my own and a couple years ago I started teachin' others around this area. Joan can come too, if you'd like. School will start up again in less than a month. I'll just need to send in for another primer for her. Won't take long."

Tears made themselves present in her eyes and Lucy did her best to force them back. "Thank you, Rose. I had been hoping Joan could get a good education."

Rose gave her a gentle smile and her eyes searched Lucy's probingly as she said, "I'd be willing to teach you too, if you need it. I've taught adults before too and there's no shame in learning, if you're wanting to."

Lucy smiled at her new friend's concern. "I've had some schooling. Nothing fancy, but I can read and write and know 'most all I need to for running a household. But thank you for the offer, I appreciate it."

"Nothing to thank me for. I just like helping people." Rose glanced to where the men were talking and leaned closer to Lucy. "So how do you like being with Garrett?"

Did she mean being with him or did she mean being *with him?* "He's a kind man. I'm blessed to have ended up with a Godly man." Lucy hoped that was a correct answer to whatever Rose was thinking of.

Rose nodded. "That, he is. Are you two, you know, romancing each other?"

Lucy blushed and her gaze dropped to her shoes.

"Well, I – We just met. W-we're not starting anything yet."

"Ah, I see. I understand how that is."

Her head came up. "You do?"

"Sure do. You see that man over there?" She nodded to her husband. "He and I weren't in love when we married either."

"You weren't?"

Rose shook her head. "I was a mail-order bride. My husband died and I was alone with little Marie to feed. I had no way to support us so I came out here as a mail-order bride. I thank the good Lord I ended up with a man like Peter Johnston. I've heard some stories about mail-order brides who fared much worse. So much danger, not really ever seeing the man you're marrying until your wedding."

"I can't imagine. I'd be too frightened to do anything like that."

"Well, your situation wasn't much different, was it?"

Lucy thought on that as Garrett and Rose's husband rejoined them. Garrett's hand sought her waist again as he drew near. Warmth spread through her and she became all too aware of his presence beside her. As well as the peculiar glance Peter threw Garrett.

"Garrett, you've got yourself a sweet little wife there," Rose announced.

Peter spoke up with a mischievous look on his face. "I'd say the same of your husband, Mrs. Black, but he ain't very sweet. Or—" he visually sized Garrett up "—very little."

A growl emanated from Garrett behind her and she giggled.

"Oh, Peter, be nice." Rose swatted her husband's arm playfully before turning back to them. "Are y'all busy today? We'd love to have you over for lunch, if you'd like."

Garrett shifted. "That's fine with me if Lucy agrees to it."

She nodded with a grin and glanced up at her husband. "I would enjoy it, yes."

"I suppose that settles it then!" Rose whirled to her husband, a sudden flurry of activity. "Will you gather up the children? I'll have to get everything ready so we should hurry home." She refocused on Garrett and Lucy. "You all can come along if you want or stay here a while longer, whatever you decide."

Garrett looked to Lucy. "I'll go get Joan," she said

His hand reluctantly relinquished her and she hurried to find Joan, her rebellious thoughts wishing she was back in her husband's possession again.

She found Joan outside playing tag with several other children. "Joan, we have to get going."

"But, Lucy, I wanna play with Hope and Andrew!" she pleaded.

Lucy smiled at her drama. "We'll be going over to their house for lunch in just a little bit."

Joan's eyes grew wide. "Really? Do you mean it?" She nodded.

"Can I ride with Hope in their wagon? Please?"

"I don't know. You'll have to ask her mama first."

"I'm going!" Joan bounded back to the house and Lucy followed. She stood back, joy filling her heart at the little girl's happiness, as Joan begged Rose for permission to ride with Hope.

"Well, I suppose so," Rose consented easily. "Long as your ma and pa agree you can."

Joan whirled on them with pleading eyes.

"That's fine with me," Garrett answered the unspoken question as Lucy nodded in consent.

"Hope! I can go!" Joan clapped her hands and the two girls scurried back outside.

Garrett's gaze seared the side of her face and she turned to meet it. The look in his eyes reminded her of an important detail – if Joan wasn't riding with them, they would be alone. And the ranch hands wouldn't be along either since they hadn't been invited. They would most likely return to the ranch. And leave Garrett and Lucy to go to the Johnstons' alone.

Refocusing on her husband, Lucy decided that wasn't a very bad idea.

Six

Garrett really didn't mind if it took them hours to get to the Johnstons' house. He set the horses at a relaxed pace and decided to enjoy his time alone with his new wife.

He wondered if he should bring up the night before but he didn't wish for her to clam up again. He wasn't really sure what to say, so he was glad when Lucy spoke first.

"I enjoyed getting to meet everybody today. It was nice. And I already know Rose and I will become good friends. She teaches some of the other children and offered to teach Joan too. I said that would be fine. Is that all right with you?"

"Yes. She should get an education. I was actually thinking of that myself."

"I think it starts next month. I don't know how she'll get there though. I suppose I can walk her there but I don't know the way."

"I can have Miguel take her to and from school."

Her eyes took on a wary gleam. "Do you trust him?"

He met her gaze. "With my life."

"And Joan's too?"

He nodded and the tension drained from her eyes.

"Good. I wouldn't be able to live with myself if something happened to her."

"Miguel won't lay a hand on her. He's quiet and a bit stern but he's a God-fearing man. He'd never harm a child."

She nodded. "He won't mind bringing her to school?"

"No. It won't take much time out of his day and I pay his salary anyway. He should be fine with it."

"Okay." She smiled.

"I'm glad that you like the Johnstons. I've been friends with them ever since I moved out here."

"When was that?"

"About three years ago. I heard about some land that was pretty cheap and snatched up the opportunity to have my own ranch. Came out here with my pa and brothers. They helped me build the house before they went home. Then I was working on the barn and stable when Peter came with a handful of other ranchers. I made a whole passel of friends that day. It took us three days to build them and by the time we were done, a bond was firmly planted. That's the kind of friendship I've always loved."

Lucy smiled up at him and the amazing feeling of such unabashed joy that he'd felt when Peter and those ranchers came to help him crept over him again. He wanted that kind of friendship with his wife too. No, something stronger. A bond that would never be broken.

"Have you ever had such friendship?" He wasn't sure where the question had come from but once he saw the sorrow that swept over her face, he wished he could take his words back.

Lucy nodded. "My brother, Travis. People say that twins are closer than other siblings and I believe it's true. We've always been able to tell what each other was thinking. I don't know if it was because of knowing each other so well or because of that unexplainable bond. I miss him. He would really like you. I know he would."

"I'd like to meet him."

"I hope you can someday. I wonder where he is."

"You last saw him in Indiana, right?"

"Yes. He was going to work for a farmer."

"So he was adopted?"

"I'm not really sure. I think so but the man seemed like he wasn't really looking for a son, but an employee."

"Hm."

"He promised to find me one day. Who knows how long that will take though." Lucy studied her hands which were folded in her lap. She looked so alone in that moment that Garrett reached out and covered her hands with one of his.

"I'm sure you'll see him again someday."

She smiled at him, a distinct sheen clouding her eyes. "Thank you."

He smiled in return and decided to change the subject. "How did you come upon Joan?"

"She was at an orphan drop somewhere in New York. She was really little at the time, two years old at the most. She looked horrible, the poor baby, and wouldn't stop crying. I took care of her and kind of adopted her myself. She's been with me ever since. I guess she's kind of like a daughter to me, though that's a strange thought." She glanced up at him and Garrett's mind filled with thoughts of having his own children and more than just adopted ones.

"What are you thinking about?"

He knew his face flushed scarlet and he ripped his gaze away from hers. "Nothing important." Except it was. Very important.

She laughed. "You're as horrible at lying as my brother is."

Garrett ignored the heat that threatened to burst into flames and teased, "Would he become a ripe tomato too?"

"No," she answered, laughter quivering in her voice. "He would get a stutter and be unable to look you straight in the eye. He got it from Father."

He chuckled and swiped a finger down her jaw. "I think you inherited some of that trait too. You start to stutter when you get nervous or scared or sad."

"I do?"

He nodded with a light tap on her chin and his eyes involuntarily flicked down at her mouth. "It's endearing."

"Oh. I-I didn't know that."

A grin spread across his face at her proof of his words. So she was nervous? Because he was touching her? He took that as a positive sign and leaned toward her. His palm cupped the side of her face and her pretty green eyes widened. He dipped his head.

"Garrett, w-what are you doing?"

The spell broken, his eyes opened and he drew back so he could see her face. Did she really not know? "I was hoping to kiss you."

"Oh." Her expression was unreadable.

"Do you mind if I kiss you?"

She turned her head away from him and his hand dropped down to his side, useless. He prayed he hadn't frightened her. Would she ever let him get near again?

"Lucy?"

She looked back at him after a moment and moistened her lips. His eyes followed the movement before returning to hers. "I-I don't think I'm ready, Garrett."

He inhaled and then released his breath, attempting to dispel the desire that made itself known. "Okay. We…I can wait."

She nodded and he turned away, just to look back at her when her hand slid on top of his. "Thank you,

Garrett. For understanding."

He didn't understand. At the very second, he was fighting the temptation to glance at her lips, to pull her close and get that kiss he couldn't stop dreaming about. He didn't understand, but he wasn't about to push her either.

He remembered Peter's warning. *"Don't take it too fast. If you do that, you'll scare her. That's one thing I learned: Never pressure a woman before her time. You won't appreciate the results."*

Garrett returned his focus to Lucy and gave her a smile. "I'll do my best to be the best husband to you that I can. Meaning your wants come before my own."

Tears glistened in her eyes and he felt like kicking himself in the gut.

"What's wrong?"

She shook her head and swiped at her eyes. "That's the sweetest thing anyone has ever said to me. Thank you."

He smiled, wishing he could wrap her in an embrace. "You're welcome."

Shrieking voices made themselves present and Garrett realized they had reached their destination – the Johnstons' ranch.

Lucy released a breath as they pulled into the Johnstons' homestead and came to a stop. She quickly climbed down from the buckboard of her own accord before Garrett could reach her.

It wasn't that she didn't want him near her. In fact, she wanted the exact opposite and it scared her. She didn't know what it was like to fall in love. Was it supposed to happen so fast? She didn't believe she was quite in love with him yet, but she certainly felt something. Was it love? And did that mean they could freely kiss? She knew they were already married so essentially it didn't matter. But she didn't want to kiss him yet. She wanted to wait until they were both in love. She didn't want to rush anything, especially since all these thoughts and feelings were so foreign. Perhaps she should ask Rose about it.

"Lucy!" She turned to see Joan dashing toward her, before darting behind her. "Andrew's chasing me!" The little boy ran forward and tagged Joan.

"You're it!" he declared triumphantly. Joan gave chase and the two raced away.

"Looks like she's having fun," a familiar voice spoke from behind her.

Garrett. "She hasn't hardly played with children her own age at all. I'm glad she's found friends so quickly." Lucy continued to watch Joan as she and the other children laughed and played.

"Wanna head inside?"

Finally she turned to look at her husband and he smiled down at her. She nodded. "That sounds like a good idea."

They headed for the house, Garrett shortening his

strides to accommodate Lucy while she hurried so they walked side by side. She was surprised when he opened the door as though it were his own house but he quickly explained that Rose would hang him out to dry if he did otherwise.

"Garrett, Lucy, come in!" Rose beckoned them with a smile. "Lucy, this is my daughter Marie." She gestured toward a beautiful young woman Lucy knew to be around her age. Her hair was a curly auburn and freckles across her nose and cheeks made her appear a few years younger. Her brown eyes, contrary to Rose's blue, smiled prettily. Lucy wondered if Marie's birth father had been a Scot.

"Hello, Lucy! Ma's told me all about you." Marie grasped Lucy's hands in excitement.

"Thank you. And hello to you too."

"So how old are you?"

"Seventeen."

"Wow. That's just a year older than me. To think I could be married that soon." Marie's eyes widened a bit and she sighed. "Sounds wonderful."

Lucy smiled at her enthusiasm. "Are you eager to start a family?"

Marie nodded. "I can't wait to have a man of my own and children too! I've been dreaming about it ever since I was little!" She glanced at Garrett. "You should be glad you got this guy cornered. I know there were a few of the other girls keeping an eye on him." She laughed and gave Garrett a hug.

Lucy hoped Garrett hadn't been keeping an eye on them too. A sliver of jealousy snaked into her heart but she did her best to banish it.

"But he's always been like a big brother to me!" Marie grinned up at Garrett and he smiled back.

"How are you feeling, Marie? Your mother mentioned that you were feeling poorly."

Marie's excitement dimmed some. "Better. Still not the best but nothing I can't handle." She gave Lucy a knowing look before glancing at Garrett and Lucy swiftly understood. Womanly matters.

"That's good. I hope you feel better soon."

"Me too. So...how do you like living with this guy?" She pointed at Garrett.

"Um...fine. I really enjoy it. Much better than the orphan train. It's already beginning to feel like home." Lucy gave her husband a smile and his eyes lit with pleasure.

"Oh, yes! The orphan train. I was wanting to ask you about that. What was it like—"

"Marie," Rose interrupted.

"Yes, Ma?"

"Lunch is ready so why don't you help me get it onto the table? I'm sure you and Lucy will have plenty of time to talk later."

"Yes, Ma." Marie headed for the kitchen.

"Do you need any help?" Lucy offered.

Rose shook her head. "No, I don't think so. There really isn't much to do. You two can just find yourselves a seat or…. Wait. You know what? There is something you can do. You can call the children in for lunch."

Lucy stepped outside and looked around for the children. Where had they gone? She descended the porch steps and scanned the area. Were they in the barn? Or did they go in the stable? Or could they be hiding behind the house? "Children," she called somewhat softly. No answer. She frowned. They were there just a minute ago.

She turned to go back inside and tell Rose when she heard a shriek followed by laughter coming from the direction of the barn. She started for the building when the six children poured out of it, laughing. Joan ran up to her, giggling hard.

"Gabriel…he fell…from the ladder…and he…and he…look!" She pointed to the boy who had muck and straw clinging to his hair and clothes. Lucy fought a smile at the mess. Thankfully, Gabriel wasn't hurt and didn't seem to mind the laughter at his expense. He teased the other children by marching toward them with open arms, threatening to share his ill fortune.

"Come on, we need to go inside. Your mother said that lunch is ready."

At her words, the children, save Joan and Gabriel, raced back to the house.

Gabriel shrugged. "Ma's gonna make me clean up first. Probably take a bath too. Good thing it's plenty warm enough to use the creek or she'd tan my hide!"

His mischievous grin almost made Lucy think perhaps the boy had fallen on purpose, just for the attention he received. "Come on, Joan. I'll race you back to the house and I'll give you a five second head start."

Joan beamed and shot toward the house. Gabriel waited the required five seconds before following. Lucy continued after them at a more relaxed pace.

She stepped into the house and her gaze automatically sought Garrett, who was standing on the opposite side of the room, talking with Peter. He glanced up and sent her a smile before turning back to Peter. Her heart gave a little tug and she covered it with her hand. Was she falling in love?

Garrett's attention veered off course when Lucy entered the house.

"So you kissed her? You actually got to kiss her?"

His head jerked to Peter. "Shh! She's right there! I don't want her to hear you and think we're talking about her."

His friend smirked. "Well, aren't we?"

Garrett ignored Peter's stab at humor and glanced at his new wife. She held her hand over her heart and was looking off into space. He wondered what she was thinking about. Whatever it was, he doubted she'd heard Peter's words.

He looked back at his friend. "No, I didn't kiss her." Frustration reflected in his tone.

"Why not?"

"I think I may have frightened her. She said she didn't think she was ready yet. I remembered what you said about going too fast and didn't try again."

Peter nodded. "That's the best thing you could have done. Forcing a kiss on her would make her think she'd married a monster and you can't undo something like that. Right now what you'll have to do is be patient. Very patient. I'm guessing right now you can't think of much else, but give it time. Wait a couple weeks before trying anything again. I've learned from Rose that women tend to work differently. They want to have an emotional relationship first before doing anything physical. So you'll have to be patient and do your best to establish that to make her happy. And, believe me, once she's in love with you, you won't find any resistance to your advances." Peter grinned. "And you'll fall in love yourself in the meantime."

"Was it the same for you and Rose?"

"Pretty close. There were a lot of things I had to learn the hard way though. I thank God Rose is as feisty as she is and wouldn't let me get away with anything." Peter smiled fondly at his wife as she exited the kitchen.

"Since Gabriel decided he wanted a bath today, we'll have to wait a little while longer before we have lunch." Rose frowned.

"Don't worry, Ma! I won't be long!" Gabriel declared before running out the door.

Garrett chuckled at the rambunctious child.

Rose approached Lucy, and Garrett and Peter walked toward them both.

"Thank you for bringing the children in, Lucy," Rose said. "I know they can be a handful sometimes."

Lucy smiled. "They were fine. All I had to tell them was that the food was ready and they all came running. And I should be the one thanking you. Joan gets along with them so well. I love seeing her so happy."

"Yes," Rose sighed. "Happy children definitely do one's heart good." She turned to include Garrett and Peter. "You can stay for supper too if you wish. We'll have plenty of time to talk."

Lucy turned to Garrett, waiting for him to answer. He shook his head. "We can't today, Rose. We plan on going to Thorn tomorrow and we need to get everything ready."

"Oh, are you visiting your parents?"

He nodded.

"They are such nice people. Don't be nervous about meeting them, Lucy. They'll love you!"

The corners of Lucy's mouth tilted upward in a smile. "I certainly hope so." She glanced at Garrett and he winked. She blushed and looked away.

"How long do you plan on visiting?" Peter asked from behind Garrett.

"We'll head back on Saturday, Lord willing."

Marie joined them. "Ma, are we gonna eat soon? Jonas is getting fussy." She nodded toward the sitting room where the children played.

"Just as soon as Gabe gets back. I sent him out a few minutes ago. He should be here any minute now."

Just as Rose finished speaking, the door flew open and a dripping Gabriel entered the house. "I'm done, Ma! We can eat now!" He grinned.

"You better dry up everything you tramp in, Gabriel Johnston," Rose instructed. "Children! Wash your hands so we can eat."

A few moments later, everyone was finally ready and sat down at the table to eat.

Seven

Joan chattered nonstop on the way home, about how Marie was so nice and Daniel was so brave and Stephen was so smart and Gabriel was so crazy and Andrew was so fast and Hope was so fun and Jonas was so little. She was quite obviously enraptured with the Johnston family. Lucy held no doubt she would fit in amazingly at school and it did her heart good. She remembered being teased in school when she was young about her mother dying and her father not being around. Any bullies who dared to tease Joan about being from the orphan train would have Rose and half a dozen children to reckon with.

Lucy looked over Joan's head to her husband whose eyes were steady on the road home. He sent her an amused glance and quirked a smile.

They'd had a wonderful visit with the Johnstons. Peter and Garrett had talked outside for a while as Lucy, Rose, and Marie socialized in the sitting room. Marie mostly asked her about what living on an orphan train was like while Rose inquired of her past life and family. After a little while, the men had come inside and they all discussed local news together. They stayed until three or four in the afternoon before deciding to start home.

"And did you know that Hope can ride a horse already? And she's younger than me. Mr. Garrett, can you teach me how to ride a horse? Please, please!"

Garrett smiled at the little girl's begging before meeting Lucy's eyes. "You'll have to ask Lucy first."

Joan swiveled toward her. "Lucy, may I? Please, oh please. I'll be real careful. Please!"

"I guess so, Joan, but you have to listen to Mr. Garrett's instructions, okay? And no doing anything silly, understand?"

Joan nodded adamantly, her pigtails swinging.

"We can start lessons once we get back from my parents' house on Saturday."

"Thank you, Mr. Garrett! Thank you!" Joan squeezed her arms around him from the side.

Garrett met Lucy's gaze for a second before looking down at Joan. "Well, since I'm gonna be giving you riding lessons and all, why don't you call me 'Pa,' Joan? It's a whole lot easier than 'Mr. Garrett'."

Lucy studied Joan, waiting to see her reaction.

The little girl grinned. "Okay, Pa."

A happy ache settled in Lucy's throat and she hoped the smile she sent her husband's way conveyed the entirety of her gratitude.

Thank You, Jesus, for bringing me here. For giving me a kind husband and for keeping Joan and me together. Thank You so much for all these blessings, Lord. You are so good to me.

They reached home a couple moments later and Garrett helped Lucy and Joan down from the wagon. Lucy led Joan inside while Garrett unhitched the horses. She went to their room.

"We're gonna have to get our clothes ready for when we go to Mr. Garrett...I mean, *Pa*'s ma and pa's house tomorrow. Here's your carpet bag. Fold up your clothes and put them in here." Lucy held the bag up to Joan, but she didn't accept it. "Take it, Joan. We need to pack up our things for our trip."

Joan stepped back and shook her head as tears clouded her eyes. Lucy approached her and knelt in front of her. She reached out and gripped her arms. "Joan, what's wrong?"

"I don't wanna pack. I don't wanna leave." Joan shook her head again and a tear rolled down her cheek. Lucy pulled her close and Joan began to cry quietly on her shoulder.

"We're not gonna leave, Joan. This is our home. We're just gonna go on a visit and Garrett is coming with us. We're not leaving, Joan." She rubbed circles on the little girl's back, tears coating her own eyes as she soothed Joan. It pained her to see what fear a life of insecurity had caused for Joan. Would she forever be afraid of traveling places?

A creak in the floorboards made Lucy look up.

Garrett stood in the doorway, concern marking his face. She wondered how long he had been there and how much he had heard.

He came forward and crouched down behind Joan. He placed a palm on Joan's little shoulder. "Joan." She lifted her head to look at him. "This is where I want you to live. You're my daughter and you'll live here with me and Lucy until you're grown and married. I want you to stay with me. Tomorrow I want to take you and Lucy to meet my ma and pa and brothers and sisters. Do you want to do that?"

Joan nodded, the tears pausing their descent down her face.

"Well, then you need to help Lucy pack what you want to bring. I'm gonna pack my things too, just like Lucy's gonna pack hers."

Lucy nodded in affirmation.

"We're just going on a visit, Joan. Me and Lucy will be with you the whole time. You want to get your clothes ready so we can be all ready to go tomorrow?"

Joan nodded.

Garrett smiled. "Then we should all get our stuff packed up. And then when we're done, we can get something ready to eat for supper."

"Okay."

Garrett rose and left for his room as Joan rubbed at her eyes. She looked up at Lucy. "Can I bring the people Pa gave me to play with?"

Lucy smiled and nodded. "I'm sure you can. Let's

get the rest of our things ready first and then you can ask Mr...Pa."

Garrett was happy to let her take them along and showed her the little pouch he always kept them in. "You can play with them on the way there too. It'll be at least seven hours so you'll need something to play with."

"We're used to traveling for long periods of time. We'll be fine." Lucy smiled slightly.

"Well," Garrett began, "what do we want for supper?"

"Flapjacks!" Joan piped up with a grin.

"Flapjacks? Those are more of a breakfast food. Why don't we have some of those for breakfast tomorrow?"

"Okay," Joan gave in.

"How about potato soup?" Lucy suggested.

"We can do that. Does that sound good to you, Joan?" The little girl nodded.

"Potato soup it is." Garrett started for the kitchen and, within the next thirty minutes, showed Lucy and Joan how to make potato soup. They chopped potatoes, boiled them along with a ham hock in water, added butter, parsley, salt, and pepper, and waited until it all cooked and thickened into a delicious soup.

Once it was finished, they set the table and sat down to eat. After Garrett gave thanks for the meal, they discussed his plans for tomorrow as they ate. Garrett wanted to have everything ready to go and leave at five o'clock. They would reach Saddle around nine and then, Lord willing, be at his parents' by noon.

"That sounds like a good idea." Lucy nodded. "You'll probably have to wake me up though. I'm not usually up yet by five."

Garrett nodded. "I can do that. Do you and Joan have all of your things ready?"

"Yes. They're all ready to go." She turned to smile at Joan. The little girl's eyes were draping shut and her head nodded sleepily. "Looks like somebody's ready for bed early today."

Joan looked up at her tiredly. "No, I'm not. I wanna stay up."

Garrett and Lucy chuckled and Garrett rose from the table and lifted the nearly-asleep Joan into his arms. Lucy followed him as he carried her into her bedroom. He gently lowered her onto the mattress and pulled the covers up over her body. "Good night, Joan." He pressed a kiss to her forehead.

"Good night, Pa." Joan held his head and gave him a kiss on the forehead too.

Lucy smiled at the pure sweetness of the moment.

Garrett backed out of the room and the two of them left Joan to her sleep.

They silently began clearing off the table and putting away the leftover soup. Lucy took the dishes to the sink and pumped water into it to start washing the dishes. Garrett finished cleaning the table and then came beside her to dry the dishes.

"I hope she won't be afraid of packing for the rest of her life."

"Me too," Garrett replied. After a moment of quiet, he added, "I don't think she will. The first couple times, probably. But each time she sees that she's really not leaving home, she'll begin to understand. I don't think her fear will last long."

Lucy sighed. "I hope you're right. I didn't realize the orphan train could leave a scar, but I suppose I should have known. She probably doesn't even remember life before that."

She continued washing and rinsing the dishes and then handing them to Garrett to dry and put away.

Garrett spoke again, his voice soft and probing. "How about you? You were on the train for seven years. What scar did it leave behind?"

She avoided his gaze and kept scrubbing at a spoon. She knew what scar it left, what fear. It was what had come up when they were in this kitchen the day before. She had avoided Garrett's questions then. Should she avoid them now?

Something inside her protested the idea. This was her husband. Shouldn't she be honest with him?

"The fear of rejection."

Her hands rested uselessly in the sink and she watched the sun slip down the sky through the window. Garrett also stopped beside her, apparently waiting for her to go on.

"Children came and went all the time on the orphan train. Some were adopted nearly as soon as they joined. Others weren't. Some of us stayed for years.

"I never did get adopted. Most people just looked me over and didn't think I was worth it. A few people actually planned to adopt me but it never happened. Th-They changed their minds." Tears stung Lucy's eyes and she couldn't stop them from coming.

"I-I even cost Joan a home before. She didn't want to go without me. The people were trying to adopt her but she wouldn't stop crying and screaming that she wouldn't leave without me. They looked at me and then at each other. They said they couldn't afford to adopt two children, so they went on to somebody else. They passed by both of us because they didn't want me."

Garrett reached for her when the sobs came. He wrapped his arms around her and held her close. His fingers massaged gentle circles into her back, silently offering her the comfort she so desperately needed.

He didn't push her away. He didn't cast her and Joan into the street. He didn't hate her now that he knew.

Her present joy mingled with the pain of the past and she wept into his chest.

Thank You, God, for letting Garrett accept me.

Her tears eventually ran out but Garrett didn't release her until her sniffles stopped too. He handed her a handkerchief.

"Thank you." She blew her nose and then handed it back to him, avoiding his face.

"Lucy, look at me."

She reluctantly obeyed.

He gazed at her tenderly. "I think you had to go

through all that, through the fear and rejection, to get to where you are now. If it hadn't happened, you and Joan probably wouldn't be together still. And I would have never gotten the pleasure of knowing you both. God has had you in His hands the entire time. And who knows what He's protected you from? Those homes could have brought you abuse or heartbreak or even more rejection. I don't know. But God always works things out for good when we love Him. And I know He's been working on things for me, or else I would have never walked into that church two days ago."

A small smile forced its way to her face. "I'm so glad you did."

Garrett once again pulled her into an embrace. "So am I," he murmured into her hair. "So am I."

Eight

"Lucy. Lucy." A hand gently shook her shoulder.

Garrett. Why is he waking me up? Is something wrong? Oh, it's Monday. Five o'clock. We're traveling to his parents' today.

She reluctantly opened her eyes. "I'm awake. I'll be up. Just give me a moment." She shut her eyes again and allowed her body rest for another few seconds while she cleared her head. She opened her eyes and saw that Garrett was still there.

He was leaning toward her slightly and watching her freely. She studied him right back, taking the time to once again note his handsome features and rugged chin. And also that he was fully dressed and looked as though he'd already been up for an hour and was raring to get started.

"Is it five o'clock?" She sat up, not sure if she should leave her bed while Garrett was there. She was in a nightgown, after all.

He nodded. "In a couple minutes."

"I'll get ready." Despite her words, she remained in place and glanced from Garrett to the door.

His eyes widened in realization. "Oh, yes. I can make sure everything else is ready. You go ahead and get dressed and wake Joan." He swiftly left the room, but not before she spotted the color climbing his neck.

She hurriedly dressed and awoke Joan. Within a few minutes, they were ready to go and soon left their bedroom to find Garrett. He was waiting for them by the kitchen and had three plates set on the table.

"Flapjacks!" Joan said excitedly, then yawned.

"Yep. There isn't much maple syrup around here so I don't have any of it, but I like to put some of my ma's strawberry jam on it and eat it like that."

Joan grinned. "That sounds yummy."

"It does," Lucy agreed.

They all sat down and thanked God for their food and for safety on their trip before digging in. Once they were finished, they cleaned their plates and forks and put them away. Finally, they gathered the rest of what they needed, and all got onto the wagon. With a flick of the reins and a click of his mouth, Garrett started the horses and they began their adventure.

Joan began talking – thankfully, to Garrett – and Lucy let her mind wander. Her husband was truly wonderful. The evening before, while she was upset and crying, he held her. He held her safe and close and at the same time, he simply held her. He didn't try anything else. He didn't press the moment to his advantage and kiss her or try to do anything that would make her uncomfortable. He simply held her close. When she was finished, he encouraged her. And when it came time for them to say good night, he gave her the same dutiful kiss on the cheek. He didn't linger, didn't try to make it a real kiss. He let her have her space, her time. He thought of her feelings first. He was the most amazing man she had ever met.

She wondered if he had learned such things from his father's example. He most likely had. His parents sounded wonderful, and as they had brought up Garrett, they had to be. If they were like her husband, she knew she had nothing to be nervous about. What characteristics came from his father and which ones came from his mother? She wished she had more memories of her own parents.

She didn't remember much of her father. But, from what she did, he was a kind man, though reserved. He often played with his children and encouraged his wife. He was always ready with a laugh and a praise. But then after her mother died, he was different. Lucy supposed he didn't know how to handle his grief. He would leave for the mountains and wander, doing what she and Travis never did discover. He came back and checked on them every week or so, then he would be gone again. They never knew exactly how long he would be gone or how long he would stay. She and Travis were able to make it fine. Travis was skilled with a fishing pole and they were able to keep up a garden. And their father would bring food for them whenever he came.

And then the storm blew in. It was huge and terrible and she and Travis were worried about their father the entire time. They would have nowhere to go without him. Then, three days after the thunderstorm, someone found him and brought him to them, dead.

Travis had always been somewhat angry at their father for abandoning them, for leaving them when his job was to protect. Lucy could never make herself very upset about it. She always saw her father as a broken man. He simply didn't know what to do after his wife died, was driven mad by the pain of it. Before he had gone off for the first time after her mother's death, Lucy had found him sitting on a log behind the house, weeping into his hands. She was never able to hold hard feelings against him because of that moment.

Her mother, from what little she remembered of her, had been a sweet person. She liked to bake and teach Lucy how to work around the house. She was somewhat of a fragile woman. She hated controversy and wouldn't argue about something unless it meant a lot to her. She loved her husband very much. Once, Lucy remembered hearing them whisper in the night. Her mother was telling him why she loved him so much. Lucy had fallen asleep before her mother was finished. Her mother loved children, especially babies. She had always wanted to have more children, but none of them lived any longer than a few months. She was delivering her sixth child when she died. The baby joined her in less than twenty-four hours.

"Lucy, why do you look sad?"

Lucy snapped out of her thoughts and met Joan's questioning gaze. "Going to visit Mr. Ga…Pa's folks made me think of my father and mother, that's all."

"Oh." Joan looked down and Lucy wondered if she remembered her parents at all. She placed an arm around the little girl's shoulders and tugged her close. She glanced up at Garrett, who sent her a small, concerned smile.

"What do you ladies think of stopping at the mercantile while we're in town? Lucy, we can get some fabric for dresses for you and Joan, if you know how to sew. If not, my ma and sisters or Rose would love to teach you."

Lucy nodded. "That sounds lovely. And I will need some help with sewing. I learned some, but not enough to make a dress."

"And Joan," Garrett continued. "Maybe we can get you a peppermint stick, if you're real good."

Joan grinned excitedly.

"How long have we been riding for?" Lucy asked.

"About a half hour. It'll be a long trip."

Lucy nodded and settled back to enjoy the ride.

Over three hours of random conversation later, Saddle came within sight as the horses kept their trotting pace. They continued to the livery, where Garrett helped each of them down and paid a boy to feed and water the horses for him.

Lucy glanced about as Garrett conducted his business with the stable hand. People milled about on the boardwalk, some simply going about their business, others stopping and talking to fellow passersby as they went. Horses and wagons traveled up and down the streets and the air was abuzz with the morning activity. The town was the same as it had been three days ago. She paused. Had it really only been three days?

Garrett's voice cut into her musings. "We'll go to the mercantile and get what supplies we need and then we can head out again. If we spend about fifteen minutes in town, we should still be at my parents' place around noon."

Lucy nodded and Joan claimed Garrett's right hand and Lucy's left. They started down the boardwalk toward the mercantile like a regular family. Which, Lucy realized, they were.

A bell jangled as they entered the store, signaling the clerk of their arrival. Several others wandered about the establishment. Garrett headed for the front desk.

"Didn't expect to see you back so soon, Mr. Black," the clerk said.

"There were some things I needed and we're heading through on our way to…"

Lucy looked around for the fabric then spotted where it was most likely to be and started in that direction. Joan tugged at her hand.

"You just stay here with Pa, okay, Joan? I'll be back in a minute. I'm gonna go look at the sewing things."

"All right."

Lucy walked to where a fancy sewing machine sat in view. The other supplies must be close by. She scanned the area and quickly located the fabrics near the corner, out of view of the registers. She approached and was soon running her hands over the pretty calicoes and patterns.

A pink with small white flowers caught her eye and she pulled it out to study it. She was sure Joan would love it. A plain gray material would make nice skirts for them both. It was sturdy too, which would be perfect for living on a ranch. She found another fabric that was white with flowers and stems in different shades of green. It would make a beautiful dress. She could see it already. A thick black material could be used for many things, possibly a split skirt if Garrett planned to teach her to ride.

Lucy startled out of her thoughts as she suddenly noticed breathing behind her. She whirled around.

Clem stood right in front of her, leaning toward her, his nearness boxing her into the corner. He grinned at her, blatant lust in his eyes. "My, you sure don't look any less pretty for havin' lived with Black."

She tried to stifle a shiver and glared at him bravely. "I must insist you move along and leave me alone, Mr. Toeger."

"Ah, I see he's put some fight into you too. That's

okay. I like my women feisty. Makes it all the better when I break 'em.'"

Lucy fought the urge to retch. *Oh Lord, help me get away from this evil man.* "Please go."

"I'd be a much better husband to someone like you than Black would. He ain't any kind of real man, not the kind a girl like you'd want." He stepped closer, forcing her back to press against the counter to keep from touching him.

"You can come with me, whether Black wants you to or not. He can't force you and if he tries, I can make up some 'accident' for him to fall into. That'll make it easier. And I don't mind that you're used goods. Don't matter to me. I may even prefer a woman with experience." Clem pressed himself up against her tightly and she turned her face away from him as he raised a hand to her neck.

Panic surged in her throat. Should she scream? Call for help? She had to get away from the vile man.

"Release my wife, Clem, and do it now."

Fury licked at Garrett's insides when he saw the fear on his wife's face as Clem forced himself at her. It took every muscle in his body to keep him from grabbing Clem and showing him just what he thought of his actions. He did his best to reign in his temper, aware of Joan standing behind him.

Clem turned to him with a triumphant sneer. "Or what?" he spat.

Without hesitation, Garrett withdrew his pistol from his gun belt and leveled it at Clem's head. "You'll do it and you'll do it now," he threatened as he cocked the gun.

Indecision warred in Clem's face as Garrett's self-control edged closer and closer to the brink. He was about ready to grab Clem and slam a fist into his wicked face when Clem stepped away from Lucy. She sagged slightly against the counter and Garrett's anger swiftly chased his relief away.

He fought to control his voice. "Leave, Clem. If I ever see you trying to put your hands on my wife again, I won't hesitate to turn you over to the sheriff or shoot you myself. Understand?"

Clem glared at Garrett for several seconds before leaving, sputtering curses as he went.

Garrett released his gun's hammer and returned it to its holster. He stepped toward Lucy as she rushed to him. She buried her face into his chest and wrapped her arms around his back. He held her close, lending her comfort and safety as he waited for the tremors shaking her body to stop. He wished Clem was there so he could make him pay for frightening his wife. He fought to bring his mind to the task at hand – calming Lucy. After a few moments, he gripped her arms and pulled away so he could see her. He eyed her, trying to determine if she was hurt.

"He didn't touch you, did he? Did he hurt you?" He would kill Clem if he dared to lay a hand on her.

She shook her head and sniffed, then met his gaze. "No. I-I'm fine."

He nodded and pulled her toward him again. He rested his cheek on the top of her head, allowing himself to smell her hair. Lucy breathed deeply and he felt her inhales and exhales against his chest. He wished he could capture the moment and save it so he could experience it anew any time he felt lonely. Instead, he savored it in the time he had.

Something brushed against his legs and he felt Joan join their circle, flinging her arms around Lucy, one of her arms separating them.

A question tugged at his mind and, after a moment, Garrett loosened the circle and looked at Lucy. "Why didn't you call me?" He would have come to her help immediately if he knew she was in need.

"I-I don't know. I wasn't even thinking, I just…"

He nodded in understanding. It happened so quickly she didn't know what to do. "If anything like that were to ever happen again, if you need help for whatever reason, call for me. I'll do everything I can to help you."

Lucy nodded.

Garrett released a breath and turned slightly to look behind her. "Did you pick out the materials you wanted?"

"Yes, but I don't know how many I should get, or how much."

"Which ones do you like?"

She showed him four fabrics and he brought the

bolts to the register as she and Joan followed. He swiftly calculated how much she would need. His mother would buy six yards for a dress for herself. Lucy was a bit smaller than her but then there was Joan as well. "May I have nine yards of each of these?"

"Of course, Mr. Black. Let me have Millie cut it out for you." The clerk fixed their order and soon had it ready to go. Garrett added it to his load of supplies.

He spotted the candy and remembered Joan. "Oh, and may I get a peppermint stick please? Somebody here is in need of one." Garrett smiled down at Joan and she grinned widely.

The clerk pulled out a piece of candy and handed it to Joan. "There you are, little lady. Just make sure you don't try to swallow it now, you hear?"

She nodded and promptly stuck the thing in her mouth. "Thank you."

They left soon after and made their way back to the livery. Garrett quickly collected the team and wagon and they loaded up their supplies and climbed aboard. Garrett set the horses in motion and they were soon once again on their journey.

Nine

By the time the team pulled into his parents' ranch, Garrett missed them so badly he wanted to jump off the wagon and run to the house he grew up in.

After returning to the trail once they completed their stop in Saddle, Lucy had asked him to tell her more about his family and one memory led to another. Within the last three hours, he had rehashed practically every memory he knew.

There was the time he somehow climbed onto a horse when he was three years old and rode to the neighbor's house. And then there was the time when he was six and he brought a flower to a girl he liked in school and then challenged his brother Richard to a duel when he found out he already gave her one. In the end, the girl gave both flowers to another girl and he and Richard became friends again. How he once told Courtney he wished she was a boy and she wrestled him until he changed his mind. How he and his brothers built a tree fort when he was ten and declared "no girls allowed" until William made an exception for the girl he liked. Then Richard and Garrett left to build their own fort, which collapsed on them a couple days later. After that, Ma disallowed them from treehouses because she'd had to stitch them up. How his sisters tried to make his favorite – apple pie – for his birthday and ended up nearly burning the house down. How he once found a bottle of the devil's brew and took a swig. He'd choked and ran to where his mother's sun tea was making and drank half the jar. His ma had demanded to know what happened and when he explained, she sent him to his father who didn't have the heart to punish him but instead asked him to never forget it and never try it again.

So many memories, good, bad, and downright hilarious. Lucy had asked for more of them until his mind came up blank. He felt like turning the question around on her, asking for memories from her childhood but most of them would probably make her sad again and that was the last thing he wanted to do.

He wondered when he'd get to see his siblings. Would they come over for supper tonight? Or would they come the next day and they'd all spend the whole day together like they used to? He couldn't wait until they arrived.

His mother stepped onto the porch before the wagon came to a complete stop by the barn. "Garrett?" She hurried toward him and he pulled her into a hug as soon as she reached him. "Garrett, what are you doing here? You didn't write us you were coming for a visit!" She turned toward the barn and yelled, "Thomas! Come here!"

"I didn't know I was coming either. But there's someone I want you to meet." Garrett nodded to the buckboard.

Ma turned and her hand flew to her mouth. "Oh my." She looked up at him. "Are you…. Did you get married?"

Garrett smiled and nodded. He stepped back to the wagon and helped Lucy down. His wife met his gaze, trepidation in her eyes. He squeezed her slightly trembling hand and gave her a reassuring smile before pulling her toward his mother.

"Ma, this is my wife, Lucy. Lucy, this is my mother, Sarah."

"Hello, Lucy. I'm Garrett's ma. How did all this come about?" Before anyone could answer, she spoke again. "Oh, what am I talking about? Come give me a hug." Ma drew Lucy to her and flung her arms around her. She pulled back after a moment, her eyes bright with tears.

"What's all the commotion?" His father approached from the barn and Garrett turned with a grin to the man who raised him. "Garrett! How are you doing, son?" The two men shared a brief embrace.

"Great, Pa. Had a surprise for the family and decided to come for a visit." Garrett nodded to Lucy.

His father's eyes widened. "My my my. Has

someone finally managed to lasso this son of mine?"

Lucy smiled. "Yes, sir. I'm Lucy, Garrett's wife."

Pa laughed and gave his new daughter-in-law a hug. "Welcome to the family, Lucy."

"And we can't forget this little girl right here." Garrett lifted Joan into the air and set her down in front of him.

His mother's eyes flicked to Lucy and then to Joan. Her eyes held a million questions. "Your daughter?"

He nodded, wondering just what she was thinking.

Ma crouched before Joan and smiled. "Hello. What's your name?"

"Joan."

"How old are you, Joan?"

"Five."

"Would you like a cookie, Joan? I've got some just waiting to be eaten."

Joan beamed and nodded enthusiastically.

Ma straightened. "Lucy and Joan, you can come with me to the house while we let the men bring your things in."

Lucy sent Garrett a small smile before following his mother. He looked to his father.

"It is wonderful to see you, son, but my mind is full of questions as I'm sure your mother's is too. You can explain while we put your horses up."

Garrett nodded. "Last Friday I went into town for supplies like I do every month and I was riding past the church when I heard some loud voices coming from

94

inside the building. I was curious so I stopped the team and went inside. When I got in there, I realized the orphan train had come through town. Clem Toeger, one of the townsfolk, was yanking a young woman, Lucy, against him when she clearly didn't want him to. I intervened and found out that if I didn't marry her, Clem would."

Garrett rhythmically unhitched the horses. "I asked her whether she wanted to marry me or Clem and she said me. And then we got hitched. Joan was on the orphan train as well. It seemed she and Lucy were inseparable and Lucy begged me to adopt her. So Joan joined the family too. That's how it came about."

His father raised a brow. "So you were rescuing a damsel in distress?"

Garrett grinned. "I suppose so. I just saw Clem scaring her and it made me so angry, I had to do something." His voice lowered as he recalled what occurred mere hours ago. "It happened again just today. We stopped in town for supplies on the way here and Lucy went off by herself to find some fabric. When we were finished with the rest, Joan and I looked for Lucy and found Clem pressing her back against a corner. I'll shoot him if he comes after her again."

Pa nodded. "I wouldn't expect anything less from a man protecting his wife. Do you think he'll try to come after her?"

"I don't know. I warned him, pulled a gun on him too, but he didn't seem particularly repentant. I should probably ask the sheriff to keep an eye on him."

"That would be a good idea." Pa led the team to the pasture and unhooked their reins, letting them free to roam. "So what else do you know about your new wife and daughter?"

"Not very much about Joan at all, except that she joined the orphan train when she was a toddler. Lucy took care of her and named her. That's why they're so close.

"Lucy has a twin brother. Their ma died when they were almost nine and after that their father went out and lived in the woods. He came to check on them regularly until there was a storm and he was killed in a flash flood. Then they joined the orphan train when they were ten, though, under her brother's instruction, she told them she was eight. He thought she would be more likely to be adopted if people thought she was younger.

"Travis, her brother, left when he was fourteen and she hasn't seen him since."

Pa sighed. "Poor girl. She probably feels like she's lost all her family."

Garrett couldn't help but agree.

"So how are you and Lucy doing? I suppose it's taking some getting used to, suddenly being married to a stranger."

Garrett nodded. "It has been different, but not very difficult so far. I like living with Lucy, introducing her to other people, showing her how things work on the ranch. She's really sweet and likes to learn, which is good because with her ma dying young she doesn't know much about cooking and sewing and stuff."

"I'm sure your ma would love to teach her."

"That's what I was thinking."

"How old is Lucy?"

"Seventeen."

Pa nodded and looked around. "Well, I'm sure there's plenty more to talk about but we can get to know Lucy more later. The womenfolk will be wondering where we are if we don't join them soon." He grabbed Joan's and Lucy's things from the back of the wagon and let Garrett get his own.

"Just one more thing, son."

"Yeah, Pa?"

"Do you and Lucy share a room? We'll need to know whether to set her up in another one or…"

Garrett shook his head. "We have separate rooms."

His father nodded. "I thought as much. Which is better until you know each other enough to take that step."

Garrett's neck warmed.

"We can get Lucy and Joan set up in Courtney's old room."

They headed for the house.

"How is Courtney doing?"

"She's fine. Just saw her yesterday. She and Sean are as in love as ever."

Garrett laughed, remembering catching them

engaged in some rather passionate kissing one time. That had been an embarrassing moment. "How about April and Ellen? I'm guessing they aren't here?"

Pa shook his head. "Nope. They stopped over at Widow Meyers' place to visit and see if she needed help with anything."

When the elderly widow had come to the area several years ago, their family had taken the responsibility of checking on her and being a friend. He was pleased to hear that his sisters still visited the kind lady.

"They should be back before too long though. They left almost an hour ago by now. Won't they be surprised?"

They reached the porch and Pa went ahead and opened the door. Garrett followed him.

His mother, his wife, and his daughter sat around the table and they all looked up when they came in. Garrett was pleased to see a smile on each of their faces.

"Well, hello, ladies, I hope you have all had a lovely visit. Garrett and I will get your things in your room for you and be back down in just a minute." Pa gave Ma a special smile and she returned it.

His father started up the stairs and Garrett came up behind him. Memories swarmed into his mind as he stepped into the bedroom he and Richard had once shared. He quickly placed his things on the bed and then found his father across the hall in his sister's room. The two men walked back downstairs and joined the women at the table.

Garrett reached beneath the table, found Lucy's hand, and gave it a squeeze. Her gaze flew to his in surprise and he smiled.

"I was just telling Lucy and Joan about how William and Heidi met," his mother explained.

Garrett chuckled. He remembered very well how his oldest brother had found his match. Once, when he was seventeen, Richard was nineteen, and William was twenty-one, they were talking and they each outlined what they hoped or expected the woman they married would look like. No more than a month after that conversation, William and Garrett had gone into town for whatever it was that they needed. They met a German man who told them in broken English that he had just moved to the area and was hoping to start a ranch. They spoke to him for a few minutes before a young woman came and started speaking to him in German. The young woman fit William's description to perfection. Blonde hair, blue eyes, even her height was what he was picturing. That was all it had taken for William.

The oldest Black son wasted no time in asking the man if he could court his niece, as she turned out to be. William and Heidi had a whirlwind courtship, during which Heidi learned English, that lasted three months before he proposed. Then they waited one more month before marrying. Though William couldn't be called the most impulsive of the Blacks, his love life most certainly was.

Well, Garrett supposed, *not anymore. I guess I beat him on that one.* How about marriage without any courtship at all?

He refocused. "When will William and Richard and their families come?"

Ma spoke up. "I was thinking you and your pa can go and visit them this afternoon and tell them to bring their families over tomorrow morning. They can stay all day and visit. And Courtney and Sean too."

"That's a great idea," Pa agreed. "We can go as soon as you're ready, son."

"I'm ready now, Pa," Garrett said with a grin. Excitement at seeing his brothers again welled. He couldn't wait until they could talk. He wondered just what they'd say about his latest news. He almost laughed just thinking about it.

Ten

"You're what? Are you serious?" William's eyes widened in shock.

Garrett nodded.

"You're really serious?"

"I am completely serious, big brother."

William's mouth snapped shut and the idea took a minute dawning on his face. "Wow! Well, congratulations!" William wrapped him in a brief bear hug. "I never would have guessed! How come we didn't know? Why didn't you tell us you were courting someone?"

"I wasn't."

"What do you mean?"

"I wasn't courting anyone. I just met her three days ago."

"Three days?" William appeared to be dumbstruck. "Wait, you didn't….Did you do one of those mail-order bride things? You know, where you write letters to someone halfway across the country. You didn't do that, did you? I never figured you to do something like that." He frowned.

Garrett shook his head, a grin tugging at his mouth as he listened to brother's musings. "No, she isn't a mail-order bride."

"Then what is she?"

Garrett stifled a laugh. He couldn't resist teasing his brother. "Well, first of all, she's my wife. And a woman. And a normal living, breathing human being."

William smacked his arm. "I *know* that. You know what I mean."

A chuckle found its way out his mouth. "I rescued a damsel in distress, as Pa would say." He explained how he found her, and Clem's despicable behavior. William scowled at the mention of it and then his face softened when he heard of little Joan. Garrett finished the story with, "And that's how I'm married to a woman I met three days ago."

William pulled a hand through his hair. "Wow. So, do you know anything about her at all? Other than that she's an orphan, I mean?"

"Of course. We haven't spent the last three days doing nothing. I'm doing my best to get to know her and figured bringing her out here to meet everybody would be a good idea."

His older brother nodded. "I'm sure Heidi would love to meet her. You know how she loves new people." He grinned and Garrett remembered her enthusiasm when meeting anyone. No one could ever claim Heidi disliked people.

"Yeah. Ma wants everyone to come over tomorrow morning and stay all day, to visit and have a good time."

"That sounds good. I'm sure Heidi will want to go right away when she hears about it, but I'll try to convince her to wait. Or maybe I shouldn't tell her until after supper, then it'd be too late to go."

Garrett shrugged. "Whatever you think is best, brother."

"Well, just be ready for guests anyway 'cuz there's a possibility we'll come for supper."

"I'm sure Ma wouldn't mind." Garrett glanced around his brother's ranch a moment. "Well, Pa and I should probably go soon. We just had to let everyone know what was going on. We're heading to Richard's next."

William looked surprised. "You haven't told Richard yet?"

Garrett shook his head and his brother's eyes lit in mischief.

"I wish I could be there to see his face when you tell him."

"If you aren't busy, you can ride out to his spread with us and just come back after. Isn't any further than three miles. Shouldn't take that long."

William nodded. "I suppose you're right. I'll come along with you." His face split into a wide smile.

"We better go get Pa then."

"Yeah, I'll tell Heidi."

The two brothers found their father playing with his

grandchildren and informed him of their plan. Soon, they were off and on their way to Richard's at a quick pace. They reached it before long and met Richard approaching from the house.

"Garrett? What are you doing here?"

Garrett swung down from his horse and the two brothers briefly embraced.

"Did you just come in? Why didn't you let us know you were coming?"

"It was a last minute decision." Garrett gave his brother a look, struggled to remain serious.

Richard's brow furrowed. "What's happened that I don't know about?"

William stepped to Garrett's side and placed a hand on his shoulder. "Our brother has done something that will change the family forever."

Wariness lit Richard's eyes and Garrett grinned. "I got married."

"Married? You got married?" Richard practically yelled in surprise and Garrett couldn't help but laugh. "Why'd you go and do a thing like that? I mean, not that getting married isn't a good thing, it's just, I didn't expect you to. I mean, not yet. Without anybody knowing or anything." Richard stopped for a moment and then gave him a mischievous smile. "So, what happened? Got bored of the bachelor life and decided to elope with one of the town girls you fancied?"

Garrett shook his head. "No. I just met her three days ago."

"Three days? And I thought William was the one with the crazy love life. How'd that happen?"

Garrett explained, with the help of William, and updated his brother on the recent events.

"So, have you kissed her yet?" Richard asked.

"I didn't even think of asking that," William mused aloud.

Garrett shook his head. "No. I haven't."

"Why not?"

"We just met, Richard. How long was it after you and Miriam met before you kissed her?"

"A couple months. But that's different. I was courting her. I wasn't married to her."

"So you'd have kissed her by now whether she wanted you to or not? Just because she's your wife?"

"Well, no, now that I think of it, I suppose I wouldn't. Does she not want you to kiss her?"

Garrett felt his neck warming. "Well, we want to wait until we know each other some. I don't want to do something I'll regret."

"That's a good idea." William nodded.

"I agree," Richard conceded. "But, you've wanted to kiss her, right? Unless, is she not attractive? I'm mean, obviously she can't be old or anything since she was on the orphan train, but is she not pretty? Not that that makes much of a difference, but, well, you know what I mean." Richard stopped talking, his face turning pink. "Well? Are you going to answer my question?"

"Question?"

"The one where he said 'But, you've wanted to kiss her, right?' before he embarrassed himself," William provided with a smirk.

Garrett laughed and Richard took a swipe at him, relieving Garrett of his hat when he ducked.

Richard huffed in impatience. "If we can get back to our original conversation, we can actually learn something here. William, you're supposed to be on my side. Don't you want to learn more about our little brother's change of fortune? Or did you learn all that you wanted when he told you?"

William shook his head, still grinning. "I'm sure there's plenty more that I haven't heard."

"And there's plenty I won't tell you," Garrett added.

"Well then, let's not waste our time. Tell us what you will tell us."

"Like what?"

"Like, I don't know, how do you live being married to someone you don't even know? I don't see how you do that. There's a lot of things I do with Miriam that you wouldn't with someone like that." Color darkened Richard's face. "And I don't mean just normal married things either. There's a lot more than that."

William nodded in understanding.

"It's not that difficult. I mean, I haven't really lived with her very long. Just a few days, but it hasn't been that hard. Yet."

"It'll probably get worse the more you get to know her, fall in love with her, and live with her without *living* with her," Richard advised.

"I know it will." Garrett sighed.

"So how long are you waiting? Until you do married things?"

"We didn't set like a certain time. Just when we're comfortable around each other. When she trusts me and wants to take that step."

Richard nodded. "So what is Lucy like? Her personality."

"She's sweet and kind of shy. She likes children. Cries kinda easy."

"Every woman does," Richard interjected and William nodded in agreement.

Garrett shrugged. "She likes to learn. I'm gonna teach her how to cook."

"She doesn't know how to cook?" Richard's mouth opened in surprise.

"No. Didn't have any way to learn on the orphan train."

"That's gonna be hard. Can she sew?"

Garrett shook his head. "She didn't have any way of learning how."

"Well, hopefully she'll learn soon, 'cuz I've seen the way you sew and nothing's gonna last long like that." Richard laughed.

"No worse than your own sewing, brother."

"That's true." They laughed. "So, when do we get a chance to meet the newest additions to our family?"

"Well, that's what we came here to tell you. Ma's

invited everyone over tomorrow after breakfast. That way everyone can meet and get to know Lucy and Joan and so they can get to know everyone else."

"Sounds like a good idea." Richard nodded. "We'll be there, probably around nine."

Garrett nodded. "Well, we should probably git. Pa and I still need to tell Courtney and Sean."

"Have fun with that." The three grinned at the thought of their newly-married and over-affectionate sister and brother-in-law. Visiting them was always amusing.

"Pa! Garrett! What are you doing here?" Courtney stepped into Garrett's arms and gave him a hug. "I didn't expect to see you!" She looked past him and cupped her hands around her mouth. "Sean! Come here!" She turned back to them with a beaming smile. "He's working on something in the barn. Probably didn't even hear you ride up. Come on inside." She ushered them to the sitting room and brought them some lemonade.

The door opened and Sean came inside. "What is it, Courtney?"

She hurried to his side and began leading him to the sitting room. "Pa and Garrett are here."

Sean greeted Garrett and Pa with a smile before they all sat down. "What brings you out here, Garrett?"

"I have a couple people that everyone needs to

meet, so I figured it was time to visit and bring them with me."

"Bring who with you?" Courtney asked.

"My wife and daughter."

"Wife and daughter? What in the world? Garrett, you're married? And you have a daughter? When did this happen?"

"Three days ago."

"Wait, I don't understand. You got married three days ago and had your daughter? Or your daughter was born three days ago?"

Garrett laughed and shook his head. "I'll explain." And he did. While Sean and Courtney listened avidly and asked questions, Pa watched the three of them as Garrett told his story.

"Wow. You're really married? That's crazy. I'm so happy for you!" Courtney stood and gave Garrett a hug. She returned to her husband and they joined hands. "And you have a daughter too! How old is she?"

"Five."

"She's the second oldest of the grandchildren then, after Hans."

Garrett nodded.

"So when can we meet Lucy and Joan?"

"Ma's invited everyone over tomorrow to spend the day there while we all get to know them," Pa said.

"I wish we could go sooner." Courtney looked at Sean.

"It would probably be best if we wait. I'm sure they

want to get settled and relax today before they meet everybody." Sean smiled affectionately at his wife and she nodded.

"That'd probably be best. Tell Ma we'll be there first thing."

Garrett and Pa stood and gave their goodbyes before heading for their horses.

"Tell Ma I'll bring an apple pie!" Courtney hollered after them as they rode for his parents' house.

Eleven

Lucy yawned as she headed downstairs. A rooster had been working hard to get her up and out of bed the past half hour and he'd succeeded. She just hoped she hadn't slept in too long. Talking with Garrett's sisters last night had kept her awake later than usual. Still, she didn't want her in-laws to think she was lazy.

She smiled as her husband's voice wafted to her from downstairs. He was speaking with his father it sounded like. Probably in the sitting room. She was tempted to go greet him and perhaps get that kiss on the cheek she missed last night, but she walked to the kitchen instead, to see if help was needed for breakfast and to see if Joan was with them.

"Good morning, Lucy!" Two voices greeted her.

"Good morning, Sarah, April," she replied and smiled at her mother- and sister-in-law.

"Joan's outside gathering the eggs with Ellen, in case you were wondering," April informed her.

"Thank you, I was. Sorry I slept in. Do you need help with anything?"

Garrett's mother waved a hand. "Please call me Ma. And don't worry about it. You were tired. The food's almost done now, but we do need someone to set the table." She handed her a stack of plates, and Lucy headed for the table.

Once the table was set, the food waiting, and Ellen and Joan inside, April sent Lucy to go tell the men that breakfast was ready. She entered the sitting room and her husband and father-in-law both stood. She smiled. "Good morning."

They greeted her as well and her face warmed at Garrett's gaze.

"I was sent in here to let you know breakfast is ready."

"We better not keep it waiting then." Thomas walked past her out of the sitting room and she and Garrett shared a smile before following.

After gathering around the table and praying, everyone got down to eating, passing the food back and forth and discussing plans for the day. They were nearly finished with their meal when a knock vibrated from the door. Ma hurried to answer it.

"Courtney! Sean! How wonderful to see you!" Hugs were exchanged and the rest of the family rose to greet them. Garrett pulled Lucy toward them.

"Courtney, Sean, this is my wife, Lucy, and my daughter Joan. And this is my sister and her husband."

Courtney swiftly gave Lucy a big hug. "Welcome to the family! I was so surprised when Garrett told me he'd gotten married. I never would have guessed but I can certainly understand why now that I see you."

Lucy smiled self-consciously and thanked her. Sean offered a hug as well as congratulations.

"Have you eaten breakfast yet? We have plenty," Ma offered

"Oh no, we're fine, Ma. Are you all eating? I'm sorry for interrupting. We can wait in the sitting room." Courtney and Sean headed into the sitting room and the rest of them quickly finished their food.

In quick work, the table was cleared and cleaned and the dishes finished. Garrett went outside with his father and brother-in-law while the ladies joined Courtney in the sitting room.

"Lucy, I want to know all about you!" Courtney said as soon as she entered the sitting room.

Lucy had a feeling she would become increasingly accustomed to her own story as she answered her new sister-in-law's questions and explained. As soon as she was finished, she diverted Courtney by asking her how she and Sean met.

"His family moved to the area during my last year of school. He and his older brother Colin were both behind in their schooling and still had some so we were in school together. Sean said he took a liking to me right away. I noticed him too but I wasn't thinking too much about boys at the time. When he got the courage to tell me that he liked me, I became interested in him too.

"After that, he tried to get to know me but for some reason something always went wrong, like if we were on a buggy ride, the wheel would come loose and fall off. Then he found out why. Sean's older brother liked me too and didn't want Sean to get in the way. Sean and his brother never got along too well, but Sean kept right on after me anyway. When he asked Pa if he could court me, Pa said yes. We had a pretty normal courtship except for Colin's resistance. He was angry at Sean until one time he came after him at a barn dance and they started a fight. Sean won and after that, Colin backed down and finally let go."

"Sean won? Is that all you're gonna say, Courtney? Sean won?" Ellen spoke up.

Courtney blushed and her younger sister continued.

"Sean won 'cuz you came in and helped him whop Colin good. Colin wouldn't have backed down if you hadn't told him to leave you alone, Court." Ellen turned to Lucy. "You shoulda—"

"Should've," April corrected.

Ellen continued, "You should've seen her out there, fighting in her fancy dancing dress. It was a sight to see." She grinned excitedly.

Courtney shrugged. "I was more tomboy than girl. I think being around Sean has brought out the woman in me." She smiled lovingly. "And I have a feeling all of the tomboy in me will be gone real soon." She winked.

Ma gasped. "Courtney, are you…?"

"In the family way?" She grinned and nodded in excitement. "I believe so."

Ellen squealed and everyone congratulated Courtney.

"I'm going to be an aunt!" Ellen beamed.

"You already are one," April reminded her with a laugh.

"I know, but now I'll be one again."

"Well, don't tell anyone," Courtney said. "I haven't told Sean yet. I want to be positive before I say anything to him, but I couldn't help but tell you all."

Lucy smiled, pleased to be included in Courtney's circle of confidants.

"How about you, Lucy? When do you think you and Garrett will be in the family way?" Ellen asked.

The ladies all gasped, and fire shot up Lucy's face.

Ellen's cheeks flushed pink. "Oh, I'm so sorry! I shouldn't have said anything. You were just talking to us last night and said you and Garrett weren't... It just came out of my mouth without even thinking. I'm sorry."

Lucy smiled. "It's all right. And I'm sure that day will come...someday." She blushed, glancing discreetly at Joan, who played with her wooden dolls and didn't seem to notice the conversation around her. She wouldn't allow herself to entertain the thought.

They all smiled and April changed the subject to the latest book she had read, *The Adventures of Tom Sawyer*.

The sound of rolling wagon wheels prompted them all to go outside, where William and his wife had arrived. Heidi quickly introduced herself, William, and their children in a clipped German accent and then gave Lucy a fierce hug. She gave Ma some *zwieback*, German bread, that she had made.

Richard and Miriam arrived just moments later and their boys leapt off the wagon and ran to their cousins. The passel of children ran off to play, Joan in their midst. Garrett's brother greeted Lucy, and Miriam followed him with a baby girl in her arms.

The men congregated by the barn while the women gathered chairs and settled onto the porch. Thankfully, Heidi and Miriam already knew Lucy's story, or most of it at least, from their husbands, so she didn't have to go over it all again.

They discussed the arrival of fall and the beauty of the changing colors of the season as well as the weather.

"Who was that young man I saw you speaking with at church on Sunday, April?" Heidi asked.

April rolled her eyes. "Clint White."

"He irritates the living daylights out of her," Ellen added.

"He finds the need to argue with me on every occasion and on every principle. And some of his ideals are so ridiculous." April's eyes snapped fire just at the thought of him. "I believe his sole mission in life is to infuriate me. That man!"

"Is he ignorant?" Ma asked.

"No. Arrogant is more like it. I just can't stand him!"

The other women smiled in amusement. Lucy got

the feeling it took a lot to get April this riled. She wondered just what this Clint White was like.

"And don't even consider the notion of he and I together. Ellen has already mentioned it and it is complete foolishness. Every aspect of the thought is purely ridiculous and the very idea makes my stomach turn. I would rather court a toad than Mr. White!" She exhaled forcefully. "Now can we discuss something else please? Perhaps a good book or Lydia's newly-acquired crawl?" She reached down and picked up her niece from her exploring of the porch to distract herself.

Heidi laughed. "I have never seen you so upset, April."

"Yes, proof that that man can do me no good!" She huffed, and kissed her niece. "So, Miriam, when did Lydia start crawling? I don't think I've ever seen her do that before. Isn't she early for crawling?"

Miriam grinned. "She's been rolling onto her belly and trying to move for a while now. Just a week or so ago, she discovered that she was strong enough to lift herself up. It didn't take her long to get moving after that."

"Six months seems early for crawling, doesn't it? Wasn't Anne just sitting up by then, Heidi?" April turned to her sister-in-law.

Heidi nodded. "But Anne takes her time with everything." She smiled down at her daughter, who stood and clung to her mother's knee.

"Each child learns at their own pace," Ma interjected.

"And Lydia's almost seven months old," Miriam added.

The baby grinned at her mother and then looked around. She spotted Lucy, who was sitting next to April, and gave her a wide-eyed look. Lucy reached out and let the baby latch on to her finger. She smiled at her. Baby Lydia sent her a drooly grin in return and leaned toward her.

"I think she wants you, Lucy." April handed her niece over to Lucy and she pulled the baby onto her lap.

"Hello, Lydia," Lucy said softly as she smoothed the baby's soft dark hair. Lydia garbled something back and smacked Lucy's leg.

Miriam smiled. "She likes you." She watched Lucy and her daughter interact for a minute. "Have you been around babies much?"

Lucy shook her head and glanced up at Richard's wife. "Children and toddlers, but rarely babies."

"You're good with them."

"Thank you."

The ladies conversed for a little while longer before Ma announced that they should start making lunch. Lucy and Ellen volunteered to watch Lydia and Anne while the rest of the women prepared the meal. Before long, the smell of delicious food floated from the kitchen. April let them know the meal was ready and asked Ellen to call in the men and children.

A few moments later, dozens of feet – big and small – pounded onto the porch and, as the door opened, the men and children poured through the entrance, chatting and laughing.

"Everybody, wash up before you sit at the table!" Ma instructed.

Garrett's eyes met Lucy's for a moment and he smiled before he left to wash his hands while Lucy returned Lydia to her mother. When the noise dropped and everyone gathered around the table to pray, Lucy found Garrett and Joan beside her.

Thomas prayed. "Dear Heavenly Father, we thank Thee for this food and pray You will bless the hands that prepared it. We thank Thee for this time we can all gather together and fellowship. We pray our thoughts and our actions would be pleasing to You. We thank Thee for Lucy and for Joan and for the void that they fill in Garrett's life, Lord. Thank You for bringing them into each of our lives. I pray that we will be a blessing to them. In Jesus' name, amen."

"Amen," the group echoed.

Twelve

Once the semi-chaotic meal was finished, the children eagerly raced for the outdoors while the men followed at a more gradual pace. Lucy helped the other women clear and clean the table. April and Ellen tended to the dishes as the rest of them returned to the porch.

"Heidi, have you gotten a letter back from your sister in Germany?" Ma asked.

William's wife shook her head, her brow furrowed in concern. "I haven't heard from her in nearly a year now. I don't know what to think. There are so many things that could have happened that I could not know about for so long."

Miriam placed a hand on Heidi's shoulder. "Maybe her letter got lost or delayed on the way here. Why don't you try sending another one?"

Heidi nodded. "I think I will do that."

"How is your uncle doing?"

"He is doing *gut*, good. He planted potatoes this

year. He thinks he'll get a decent crop from it."

"That's good."

April and Ellen joined them a moment later.

"Did we miss anything interesting?" Ellen asked.

"Wir sprachen uber meine Schwester und mein Onkel." Heidi replied in German, which Lucy didn't understand a bit of. April smiled.

"Do you know what I said?" Heidi asked, this time in English.

"Some," April said. "You said something about talking, your sister, and your uncle."

Heidi nodded. "I said 'We were talking about my sister and my uncle.' You are learning very fast."

"Thank you." April smiled.

"You're learning German, April?" Lucy spoke up.

She nodded. "Heidi's teaching me."

"Just High German. There are different dialects in different parts of Germany. This is High German, which is what most Germans speak," Heidi explained. "And when April learns, I will have another person to speak it with. I don't want to forget."

"My parents were from France. They both spoke French and I learned some, but I don't remember it anymore." Lucy wondered if Travis remembered any of the French they were taught.

Ellen piped in with a grin. "Well, my parents taught me English when I was a baby and I still haven't forgotten how to speak it."

Laughter flowed from the group at Ellen's quip.

"Where's Courtney?" April asked once the mirth had died.

Lucy glanced around and then stood. "I'll go see if she's inside."

"Oh, you don't have to. I can check." April got to her feet.

"No, it's fine. I was wanting to get a drink of water anyway." Lucy waved her down into her seat. "I'll be back in a minute."

She stepped through the maze of women and headed for the door. After opening the door, she walked inside and headed for the kitchen. After her drink of water, she set about to find Courtney. She didn't see her in the dining area. Maybe she was relaxing in the sitting room.

She crept toward the entrance quietly in case Courtney had decided to take a nap. She peeked into the room.

Heat seared her face when her mind registered what she was seeing. She stifled a gasp and quickly jerked back away from the entrance. The last thing she'd expected was to find Courtney and Sean kissing. She turned to go back outside and saw Garrett standing just inside the house. He grinned, stepped toward her, and grasped her hand, pulling her into the kitchen.

"Did you catch them?" he asked softly.

"What?"

"Did you catch Courtney and Sean kissing?"

She nodded, her cheeks still warm from the incident.

Garrett grinned. "I think every single one of us has found them doing that at least once. Good thing they didn't see you. Then it would've been worse."

She smiled. "It definitely surprised me."

"You know," Garrett murmured, moving closer. "I think I'm indebted to you."

Her eyes widened. "What do you mean?"

His hand slipped to her waist and pulled her near. "If I remember right, I owe you a kiss from last night."

"Oh." Yes. Her kiss.

"Unless you don't want it."

"N-No, I do." Very much so, though she wasn't going to admit it to him. Not now anyway.

He bent his head and his breath warmed her face a second before his lips brushed her cheek. He pulled back a notch and they stared at each other for a few blessed moments. Then he glanced down at her mouth and then back at her eyes. She prayed they didn't reveal her true feelings because if they did, he would see she didn't have any willpower to resist a real kiss.

The door banged open and Garrett stepped back as Joan ran inside. "Lucy, Lucy, come quick! Hans is hurt and it's all my fault! I didn't mean to do it! Oh, Lucy, come fast! He's hurt! I need water!" She grabbed a glass and Garrett helped her pump water into it.

Joan dashed outside with the water and Lucy and Garrett followed to where everyone huddled over the ground by the barn. William knelt beside Heidi, who sat with a still Hans in her arms. She patted his cheeks.

"Hans, Hans, *wek auf*! Wake up! Wake up please."

Joan gave William the cup of water and he splashed it onto his son's face. Hans jerked and coughed. His eyes opened as breath returned to him. Heidi clasped Hans to her and looked upward. "*Danke, Gott, danke.*" William joined the embrace, wrapping his arms around his wife and son.

Everyone released a breath and thanked God for giving Hans another chance.

"What happened?" asked Courtney, who stood beside Sean.

Joan faced everyone with tears in her eyes. "It's all my fault. Hans said he could walk across the stable door without falling and I told him he couldn't do it. So he went up there and tried to prove me wrong and then he fell. It's all my fault. I shouldn't have told him that."

Heidi lifted her son's chin to make him meet her gaze. "You tried to walk across the stable door? Hans, you know better than that! How could you do something so foolish?"

Hans looked down at the ground, properly chastised.

William turned to Joan. "It isn't your fault, Joan. Hans knows not to do something so reckless. It's his own fault."

Joan sniffled, wiping at her face, and nodded. "Yes, sir."

Hans was assigned to his mother's side for the rest of the day, both as a punishment and so Heidi could keep an eye on him and make sure he was all right, Lucy suspected. Thankfully, the boy showed no signs of internal damage and the day continued.

After supper, the sky began to dim and goodbyes and hugs were shared, as first Richard and Miriam left with their children, and then William and his family, and lastly Courtney and Sean. Joan went to bed soon after and then Lucy and Garrett stayed up for a while talking with his parents and sisters before they each retired to their bedrooms for the night.

Thirteen

Lucy smiled and waved back at Thomas, Sarah, April, and Ellen as the wagon continued forward. They were unrecognizable figures on the prairie by the time she turned around. She sighed, knowing the memories made from the last few days would stay with her for a very long time.

"Did you enjoy visiting my family?" Garrett asked from the seat beside her.

She turned to look at him, her back to the rising sun. She smiled. "I did. They're wonderful people."

He smiled and returned his attention to the team in front of him, apparently satisfied.

Joan returned to dreamland in the wagon bed, but Lucy was wide awake as she pondered the last few days.

The first thing that came to her mind was the conversation she'd overheard between Garrett and his mother Monday night. Lucy had been looking for Garrett to ask him if he wanted to say good night to

Joan before she went to bed. He and his mother were outside on the porch talking and Lucy didn't wish to interrupt them.

"Garrett, how...how well do you know Lucy?"

"As well as I can for knowing her for three days, I guess. Why do ask, Ma?"

"A mother has her concerns." Sarah sounded hesitant.

"What concerns, Ma? Are you afraid she isn't the one you've been praying for these twenty-four years?"

"No, Garrett. Lucy is wonderful. She truly is. I already love her like a daughter. I just...Is Lucy a Christian, Garrett?"

"Is that all you are concerned about, Ma? Yes, she is. I suspected she was from the very beginning and that was one of the things we discussed on our way here."

"I'm happy to hear it, son. It's just.... I've heard so many stories about orphans. You know I don't hold any prejudices, but they can't all be untrue. It just worried me."

"I know, Ma. But don't worry. God has truly blessed me with Lucy."

Lucy supposed she couldn't fault her mother-in-law for her concerns. Truly, there were many orphans that gave the rest of them a bad name. She personally knew of several who wouldn't think twice about swiping someone's belongings. It would be odd if nobody questioned them. It warmed her heart to hear her husband's defense.

On Tuesday morning, Garrett had announced that he wanted to spend more time with his siblings. His plan was to spend each day – from after breakfast 'til dark – at one of his brothers' or sister's place and then returning to his parents' for the night. Tuesday at William's, Wednesday at Richard's, Thursday at Courtney's, and then back to his parents' on Friday. The idea had worked out well.

Lucy enjoyed getting to know her new German sister-in-law. Heidi told her about how her life had been in Germany and how she crossed the great Atlantic Ocean on a ship with her uncle and his family. Turns out, Heidi was an orphan too. She explained how she had met William and barely knew enough English to say her vows when they got married. She told Lucy stories of her and William's many trials and triumphs over their seven married years. And she let Lucy in on a secret – she was with child. William already knew but they decided not to announce it to everyone until the first dangerous three months were out of the way. "But you won't be here by then, so I can tell you early. Just wait until you're back home to tell Garrett, unless William's already told him. Wouldn't want it to accidentally get out."

Heidi also gave her the recipe for her yummy *zwieback*. Lucy hoped to try to make it sometime.

On Wednesday, Miriam engaged Lucy's and Joan's help in harvesting vegetables from her garden. As they worked, Lucy learned her love story.

Miriam had lived in the area nearly her entire life and had pretty much always liked Richard. She saw him at church but could never work up the nerve to go up and talk to him. One time, when she was twenty, she'd found Richard injured beside the road and drove him to the doctor in town. He had been taking a new wild young horse out for a ride when the horse had spotted a snake and startled, unseating him. The horse took off while Richard, his hand caught in the reins, was dragged behind. He finally managed to loosen himself and that's how Miriam had found him. Thankfully, he was able to walk away from the injury with only bruised ribs, and some bumps and scrapes. And a curiosity for Miriam. They were officially acquainted soon after that and it wasn't long until they were courting and married about a year later.

Lucy was able to see baby Lydia as well, who preferred to be held by her more than anyone else, other than Miriam, of course.

The next day, Courtney had given her a tour of their house while Garrett worked outside with Sean. Courtney taught her some basic sewing and regaled her with childhood stories – most ones that Garett had already told her, but some of them were new. Courtney showed her how to make a hearty beef stew. She also asked Lucy more about herself and soon knew nearly as much about her as Lucy knew about herself. She also provided Lucy with what she found to be the greatest guide to romance. Forgive him when he acts like an idiot, and kiss often. Lucy decided not to comment on that one.

On Friday, April and Ellen took Lucy with them to

town, so April could see if the general store had any new books and so Ellen could ask about the annual dance coming up. Ellen had chattered about how she could hardly wait for the dance and what boys she hoped would be there. April had simply shaken her head at her sister's ideas, and managed the team.

Next, they'd taken her to an elderly widow's house. The woman had been extremely pleased to meet her and told her all about how she had met her husband and how he fought in the Mexican War and she and her sister were nurses at the hospital he came to. She slipped a note into his pocket when he was unconscious and later, after he'd left the hospital, he found it. He came back for her once the war was over and they courted and married. Then she told her about their five boys who all fought for the Confederacy during the War Between the States and three of them died. She'd told Lucy about how each of them died, the other sons' returns and marriages, the death of her husband, and how she'd moved there. She seemed to tell Lucy of her life's every detail up until the current moment. They left after visiting with her two hours and then headed home.

After supper, April and Lucy had a chance to talk. April had asked Lucy if she'd ever had any big plans for the future that felt so impossible and yet she'd never stop reaching for them. Lucy wasn't sure how to answer – she'd only ever wanted to be loved and cherished – which, at times, felt impossible but not anymore. April had revealed her secret dream to Lucy – to become a writer. She wanted to write books, like Jane Austen and Charles Dickens and Mark Twain. She wasn't sure how and had no idea of where to start, but she wanted to try.

"I have stories that appear out of the air and stay in my brain. Stories for books, stories that people would love to read. I want to write them. I feel like I have to, or they'll never get the opportunity to speak and touch lives." A passion had burned like fire in April's eyes. "I feel like that's my calling. Don't tell anyone. I haven't really told anyone else, but I've been thinking about it so much lately and I was telling you before I knew what I was doing. Thank you for listening. Just please, don't tell anybody."

Lucy had promised to keep April's secret and encouraged her to follow her dream, or to at least try.

And today, Saturday, was passing with the speed of a shooting star. They were up and had everything packed by breakfast time and then started for home after the meal.

Lucy enjoyed visiting Garrett's family and getting to know them. She supposed that now they were her family too. A smile formed on her lips at the thought. If she were ever to choose her own family, it would definitely be them.

She was ready to return to Saddle though, and the ranch that was beginning to feel like home.

Fourteen

As September dawned and the summer heat began to fade, Joan and Miguel mounted his horse each morning and rode out to the Johnstons' place for school. It took Lucy a while to get used to being at the house alone for hours, without her little friend, now her daughter, by her side. But she kept herself busy by teaching herself how to sew, tending to the garden, and reading Garrett's Bible. Joan returned with Miguel every afternoon with tales of school and her new-found fascination with Garrett's Mexican foreman.

"Did you know Mr. Miguel has a son, Mama?" Joan asked one afternoon, her eyes nearly as wide as the tea saucers at the mercantile. Lucy smiled. Joan had begun to call her "Mama" and, though it was strange to her ears at first, she loved the sound.

"No, I hadn't heard that."

"Me neither, before Mr. Miguel told me. He said he was born out of a lock or something and he can't see him."

"A lock?"

Joan nodded. "Mm-hm. A lock that's got something to do with bein' fed, or a bed, or something."

Did she mean wedlock? Lucy wasn't sure she wanted anybody educating Joan on the sins of the world. She'd learn about them soon enough. Maybe she should speak with Garrett about Miguel taking Joan to school. If he was a bad influence on her, Lucy didn't want innocent Joan to be around him.

"What else did he say about it? You said he can't see him?"

"Uh huh, 'cuz Tim-o-te-o, that's Mr. Miguel's son, his mama's father won't let him. He said he doesn't like him 'cuz he doesn't have any money. Tim's mama's pa is real rich, he said, and he doesn't like Mr. Miguel 'cuz he isn't rich."

"You know that's wrong, right, Joan? You know that it's wrong to judge someone because of their money, whether they have a little or a lot? It's what's inside their heart that matters."

Joan nodded. "I know, but that man doesn't. Maybe you should go tell him that, Mama, so then maybe he'll stop shooting at Mr. Miguel."

Shock filled her. "Shooting at him?"

"Yup. He shoots at him and makes him leave his property or else he'll call the sheriff. That's why Mr. Miguel never gets to see Tim. 'Cuz his mama's pa always shoots at him and makes him leave. He isn't a very nice man." Joan shook her head sadly.

"No, it doesn't seem like he is," Lucy said. "But, you should still pray for him. Jesus says to love our enemies and to pray for them too."

Joan looked up at her. "Do I have to?"

She stifled a chuckle. "I think you should."

Joan sighed and then scrunched her eyes closed. Her lips moved slightly but Lucy wasn't able to make out what she was whispering. She opened one eye and peeked at Lucy. "Is it all right if I ask Him to make Tim's mama's pa nice so Mr. Miguel can see his son again?"

Lucy nodded, a smile tugging at her lips. "That is perfectly fine, Joan."

Joan shut her eyes again and then popped them open a moment later. "Okay. I'm done."

Lucy smiled. "Why don't you put your slate away and wash up for supper then? You can tell me how school went when you're done."

Joan started for her room then stopped and turned back. "Mama?"

"Yes?"

"Why does Jesus want us to love our en'mies?"

"Because Jesus wants us to love everybody, even those we don't like. That's why He came to Earth and died on the cross for us – to show us that He loves us. And so that we can love others."

A wrinkle formed between her eyebrows. "How come He had to die to say He loves us?"

Lucy knelt in front of Joan and met her gaze. "Well, God is perfect and He created us, but we sin and do bad things and aren't perfect like He is. God lives in Heaven and He loves us and wants us to live with Him too but we can't because nobody can go to Heaven with sin on them. That's why Jesus, God's Son, came to Earth. He became a man and was killed and died on a cross for us. Because we can't get to Heaven by ourselves, He died and then rose from the dead so that if we believe on Him and accept Him into our hearts, we can go to Heaven to live with Him and with God when we die."

Joan's eyes were wide and serious. "But what if you don't 'cept Jesus into your heart?"

"Then you go to Hell. Since God can't have sin in Heaven, if you don't let Jesus save you and wash you clean from your sins, the only other place for you to go is Hell, where you have to pay for your sins. But if you do accept Jesus into your heart, then you can go to Heaven because He already paid for your sins for you when He died."

"Did you do that, Mama? Did you 'cept Him into your heart?"

Lucy smiled. "Yes, I did, sweetheart. When I was just a little bit older than you."

Joan nodded. "How do you 'cept Him into your heart, Mama? I wanna live with you and Jesus when I die."

Tears stung Lucy's eyes. "You just ask Him to save you and forgive you of your sins and believe that He already has."

Joan closed her eyes and whispered, "Jesus, can You please save me and forgive my sins? I wanna 'cept You into my heart. And I wanna live with You in Heaven. Amen." She looked up at Lucy. "Why are you sad, Mama? Now I'm gonna live with you and with Jesus when I die."

"I know, Joan. I'm not sad. I'm happy." Lucy pulled her into a hug. "I'm very happy."

After supper, Lucy turned to Joan. "Was there something you wanted to tell Pa, Joan?"

Joan looked up at Garrett with a grin. "I 'cepted Jesus into my heart today. Mama told me how."

Garrett's face lit with joy. "You did? That's wonderful, Joan. You made Jesus very happy today."

"I did?"

He nodded. "Jesus loves it when you trust in Him because He wants you to live in Heaven with Him."

"Are you gonna live with Him too, Pa?"

Garrett smiled. "Yes, I am."

Joan beamed. "So that means I'll live with you and Mama and Jesus in Heaven! Do you think Mr. Miguel is gonna live with us in Heaven too?"

He frowned. "You know what? I'm not sure, Joan."

"That's okay. I'll ask him later."

Lucy remembered her plan to discuss the foreman with Garrett. "I think it's getting close to bedtime now, Joan."

They kissed Joan good night and she left to tuck herself into bed. Lucy explained to her husband what Joan had told her.

Garrett nodded. "I knew about Miguel. Not too much, but enough. I like to know some about the men before I hire them. And he's shared some things with me. He gets a weekend off every once in a while and when he came back beat up a few times... Well, he was obligated to let me know why."

Lucy gasped.

"Miguel doesn't have the cleanest past. If you want someone else to walk Joan to school, I understand. I can arrange it."

"No, no, I don't have a problem with him walking her, I just don't want her to learn about...all that. She's only five and so innocent. I don't want her to learn about the sin out in the world. At least, not yet."

Garrett nodded in agreement. "If he keeps mentioning it, I can let him know that we would rather he didn't talk about it with Joan. I'm surprised that he did anyway. He barely wanted to tell me anything."

"He probably trusts her and knows she won't judge him for it. And Joan may have asked him. She can be rather curious."

Garrett smiled fondly. "I can't tell you how pleased I am that Joan accepted Christ."

Lucy sighed. "I know. I feel the same. I'll never forget it."

He shook his head. "That's every parent's dream, I

think. To know their child is going to Heaven."

"I agree."

Garrett's jaw stretched wide in a yawn. "Well, I should get to bed before I end up sleeping right here. But remember." He met her gaze in a mock stern manner. "Horseback riding lessons tomorrow."

She nodded bravely. She had agreed to let Garrett teach her how to ride a horse. She was a rancher's wife after all, and Joan already knew more about riding a horse than she did. It was time to put her fear behind her and learn. "At three? Once Joan's back from school?"

"Yep." Garrett smiled. "You'll learn how to ride a horse once and for all." He stood and stretched. "But for now, we both need to go to sleep."

Lucy got to her feet and allowed Garrett to pull her near. He pressed his mouth to her cheek as he did every night. She smiled. He was so sweet and gentlemanly. Impulsively, she caught him before he straightened away from her and touched her lips to his cheek. She stepped back, out of his reach, and sent her husband a small smile. "Good night, Garrett."

Pleasure warmed his eyes. "Good night, Lucy."

Wearing the divided skirt she'd sewn for herself, Lucy felt ready to put her fear of horses to the test when Joan, who had insisted they wait until she was there, jumped down from Miguel's mount.

"Wait for me, Mama!" Joan dashed inside the house, most likely to put her lunch pail and slate away.

Garrett appeared out of the barn leading Honeysuckle, an older Palomino mare. Lucy approached the horse and gently stroked its head.

"I'm gonna ride you today, Honeysuckle. Please don't throw me off," she whispered into the mare's ear.

The door slammed shut and Joan rushed to her side. "You're gonna love Honeysuckle, Mama. She's a real good horse. I rode her all over almost. But now I can move on to the next one, Pa says. I'm good enough so I don't need a slow horse anymore. But she'll be real good for you, Mama. Just 'member to hold on tight, but not too tight or she'll think you want her to go fast. Just tight 'nough so you don't fall off or nothin'." The little girl beamed.

"Thank you for the advice, Joan. I appreciate it." Lucy turned to her husband. "How do I get on?"

Garrett hitched Honeysuckle to a fence post and then crouched beside the horse, his fingers weaved together. "We don't have a mounting block. You can just use my hands as one."

"Oh. But I don't want to hurt you."

Garrett smiled. "It won't hurt a bit. Just hold on to the pommel and place your left foot in my hand and swing your right leg up and over Honeysuckle's back."

Praying the horse would stay still, Lucy grabbed the pommel and stepped into Garrett's hands. He lifted her foot up to aid her as she swung her other leg over the saddle. Once she was securely seated, she sent her husband a smile. "I did it!"

He grinned. "Yes, you did." He showed her how to put her feet in the stirrups before he unhitched Honeysuckle. "I'm just gonna lead you around first, okay?"

She nodded. "Should I hold on to the pommel or her mane?"

He shrugged. "Whichever you want."

She clung tightly to the pommel as Garrett turned the horse around and began walking. Joan hurried to catch up with him and stayed by his side. "Isn't it fun, Mama?"

Lucy nodded. "Um, yes, it is."

Garrett led Honeysuckle at a walk for a few minutes as Lucy became used to the slow gait and relaxed her grip. He brought her to an empty corral close to the barn. He looked up at Lucy. "Do you think you're ready to ride on your own?"

"On my own?" Tension raised her voice.

"I'll walk beside you, but you hold on to the reins. You can just walk her. I'll be ready to grab the reins if anything happens."

"Okay. I think I can do that."

Garrett opened the gate and led Honeysuckle into the corral. "Joan, stay at the gate." He stopped and handed Lucy the reins.

"What do I do?" she asked, holding them awkwardly in her hands.

"Just kick her side a little to get her to go. If you pull the right rein toward you, she'll turn right and the same with left. Pull back on the reins to make her stop. And just squeeze your legs or give her a kick to make her go faster."

Lucy nudged Honeysuckle's side with her foot. The horse didn't move. She tried again with a bit more force but still, Honeysuckle didn't budge.

"Don't be afraid to kick her, Lucy. She's over a thousand pounds of muscle and fat. You won't hurt her."

Lucy was more afraid of being hurt by her, but she didn't say anything. She tried again and Honeysuckle started walking slowly. Garrett strode beside the horse, keeping even. Honeysuckle slowed until she was at a stop again. She immediately began to graze.

"Get her walking again and speed her up a bit, so she doesn't have time to eat," Garrett instructed.

Lucy nudged Honeysuckle back into a walk and then again, letting the horse's strides lengthen.

"Good. Now turn her to the left."

Lucy pulled on the left rein and Honeysuckle immediately changed direction.

"Great." There was a smile in Garrett's voice.

She grinned, proud of her accomplishments.

A scream rent the air from behind her and Lucy jerked the reins to the left. *Joan!* Startled, Honeysuckle bolted in the opposite direction. Lucy fought to keep her seat, clenching the reins with all her might. "Whoa,

Honeysuckle! Stop! Whoa!" She struggled to sit up and get a better grasp on the reins and lost her hold.

The ground rushed up to meet her as she landed hard on the ground and rolled. Hoofbeats pounded away as footsteps rushed closer.

"Lucy!" Suddenly Garrett was kneeling beside her, Joan on the other side. Garrett pushed her hair away from her face. "Are you all right? What hurts?" Concern darkened his eyes, his mouth drawn into a thin line.

Pain made itself known from her arm, head, back, all over her body. She groaned. "Joan? I heard you scream."

Tears ran down the little girl's face. "It was just a wasp, Mama. It scared me. I'm sorry, Mama. I know I shouldn't have screamed."

Relief that Joan wasn't injured swelled, as well as the pounding in her head.

"Lucy." Garrett leaned toward her and she met his gaze. "Where is the pain coming from?"

"I-I don't know. All over. My head, and my arm, and my back."

Garrett nodded. "I'm going to see if I can feel any…broken bones or injuries. Tell me if anything hurts."

He ran his hands down her shoulder and arms then again down her sides and legs. Nothing was especially painful so Lucy kept silent.

"You seem fine. How did you land?"

"On my side. I rolled."

"How is your head?"

"Pounding."

He moved closer to her and gently inspected her scalp. She cried out when he reached it. His fingers immediately left. "I'm sorry. There's a scrape on your head."

"I know," she managed.

"Do you feel tired? Or sick?"

"Not really."

Garrett let out a breath. "I'm going to carry you inside, all right? It'll probably be painful." He slipped one arm beneath her knees and the other under her shoulders, studying her face for signs of pain.

She bit her tongue to keep quiet but couldn't silence a moan as he lifted her off of the ground. Garrett hurried to the house as Joan ran beside him. He strode into the house and slowly lowered her onto her bed.

Garrett's voice was low. "Joan, please get one of the cowhands and tell them to ride for the Johnstons' and bring back Rose."

"But—"

"Now, Joan. Please. If no one's in the barn, check the bunkhouse."

Little footsteps rushed out of the house.

Garrett smoothed Lucy's hair out of her face. "Do you want some water?"

She nodded and instantly regretted it. "Yes."

He left and brought back a glass of water and a wet washcloth. "Do you think you can turn your head? I think we should probably clean out the scrape on your head, but I don't know if I should wait for Rose or do it myself."

Lucy wanted to wait until Rose could do it so Garrett wouldn't see her cry, but she knew that was foolish. "I don't want Joan to be here." If the little girl was already blaming herself, seeing Lucy's pain would only make it worse.

Garrett nodded. "I suppose I'll do it now." He stood beside the bed and paused, seeming unsure of what to do. "Do you think you can sit up?"

"I can try."

Garrett slid a hand beneath her and helped to slowly lift her into a sitting position. Lucy fought against the nausea that rolled through her.

"Go ahead."

Garrett lifted the damp washcloth and, after hesitating, dabbed it gently onto her wound. She sucked in a sharp breath. He did it another couple times before pressing it onto her scrape. Tears pooled into her eyes and she couldn't stop the cry that rose in her throat.

Garrett stopped and looked into her face. "I'm so sorry, Lucy. I don't want to hurt you. Maybe I should wait for Rose."

Lucy blinked through the moisture in her eyes, focusing on her husband. "No-No, it's all right. Please finish. I want it to be over when Joan comes back inside."

He nodded and returned to his task. Lucy managed to keep silent through most of it, knowing that hearing her pain hurt Garrett as well.

Joan ran in just after Garrett had lowered her back onto the bed. "Rose is here, Mama!"

Fifteen

Garrett nearly sagged with relief when Rose walked through the door. Hearing Lucy's cries and seeing her tears – knowing he was causing them – was too much to deal with. He would gladly turn her care into Rose's capable hands. He couldn't stand to see her suffer.

Rose hurried to Lucy's side and launched into work, asking questions and drilling out orders. An hour later, Garrett and Joan had helped to bring ice, wrap bandages, and make sure Lucy stayed awake.

The full extent of her injuries was the gash on her head, a nasty bruise on her shoulder and collar bone where she had most likely landed on a rock, and various scratches and bruises on her arms, legs, and face. Rose advised her to stay in bed for a couple of days just to be sure that her head wound wasn't too serious and to stay off of a horse until she was completely healed, which could take about two weeks.

Rose left after telling Garrett to keep Lucy awake for

two hours and to come get her if he thought anything was wrong.

The rest of the day dragged by as Garrett kept Lucy awake for the required two hours and then watched her sleep. The next thing he knew, he heard Joan's voice. "I think he's sleepin'. He probably stayed in here to make sure you don't fall 'sleep and hurt yourself. Should I wake him up?"

Garrett opened his eyes. "No need. You already did." A yawn nearly cracked his jaw.

"Pa! I didn't know you were awake! Why didn't you tell us?" Joan came to the side of his chair.

"I didn't know I was awake either until just a second ago." He looked past her to Lucy. "How do you feel?"

"Okay." She smiled a little. "My head's still kicking up a fuss but it's all lessened for the most part."

"Good. Well." He glanced down at Joan. "Should we go make up some breakfast?"

"Mm-hmm. And then I can bring some to Mama and feed it to her."

"I'm sure I can feed myself, Joan."

Garrett, with some help from Joan, cooked oatmeal for the three of them. They all ate in Lucy and Joan's bedroom.

Lucy insisted that Joan go to school and soon the little girl was waving from the front of Miguel's horse as they rode to the Johnstons' homestead.

Garrett was unsure if he should stay inside with Lucy or go work on the range. Perhaps he should ask her.

"Go work, Garrett. It'll probably drive you crazy to stay in here all day." She smiled. "I'll be fine by myself. Just wait. In a week or two from now, I should be completely healed."

Turned out, she was right. Two days later, she was out of bed and able to walk around without hurting her head too much. Within a week, all that remained was soreness. And, other than the bruise that still darkened her shoulder, Lucy was continuing normal life less than two weeks later.

One day, without prompting from Garrett or Joan, Lucy announced her desire to try to ride Honeysuckle again. Garrett was pleased to see her perseverance. Less than three weeks after their initial lesson, Lucy received her horse riding lesson number two, this time completely painless.

Life fell back into its familiar rhythm as the sun began to descend earlier in the evening and the wind held a bite. September faded into October and the temperature began to drop. School continued and Garrett and Lucy were pleased to hear that Joan did very well in her studies and had many friends. Joan loved to come home and regale Lucy with tales she learned from Miguel, one of her best friends. In the little girl's eyes, there was nothing the foreman could do wrong. Garrett's work on the ranch continued as the cows were brought to nearer pastures in preparation for winter. So far, Lucy had sewn two dresses for herself as well as two for Joan. She began sewing a jacket for Joan so she'd be plenty warm while traveling to and from school.

That night, Joan had a question. "Pa, Hope asked me if I could sleep at her house. Do you think I could?"

Garrett took a swig of his coffee. "Sleep at her house?"

Joan nodded. "Just for one night tomorrow. And then I could come back after school. Can I? Please? Hope already asked her ma and pa and they said yes."

"Oh, they did, did they?" Garrett glanced at Lucy, his brow arched in amusement. "What do you think about that, Lucy? Has Joan been a good girl?"

Lucy grinned. "I think so. Though there still are some scraps she forgot to take out to the chickens today."

Joan gasped. "I'll do it right now!" She ran to the kitchen and then back out the door.

Garrett and Lucy laughed.

Little steps pounded on the porch and Joan hurried back into the sitting room. "I did it, Mama! Now can I go? Please?"

"Well, now that those scraps are taken care of, I don't see why you can't go. What do you think, Garrett?"

"That sounds reasonable to me. On one condition."

Joan leaned against his legs. "What is it?"

"You give me a kiss first." Garrett tapped his cheek.

Joan grinned, stood on her tiptoes, and smacked a kiss on Garrett's cheek. "Thanks, Pa!"

"You're welcome."

"You better make sure you get your chores done

tomorrow morning before you go," Lucy reminded. "And I'll be wanting one of those kisses too."

Joan giggled, climbed onto Lucy's lap, and pecked her on the cheek. Lucy returned it and gave her a squeeze.

Garrett smiled at his girls. After the last two months, he couldn't even remember how he got by without them. How could you love someone so quickly?

"It's getting to be about bedtime for you, little missy."

"But, Mama—"

"No '*but, Mama*s.' You'll probably stay up till who-knows-when tomorrow with Hope. You can get a good night's rest tonight."

Joan sighed. "Yes, Mama." She walked to the bedroom door before turning around. "Good night."

"Good night, Joan." Garrett and Lucy replied in unison.

The little girl entered the room and shut the door.

Garrett turned to study Lucy, who had returned to her task – sewing Joan's jacket.

"When is Joan's birthday?"

Lucy's head popped up. "In truth? I have no idea. I always considered the day we first met to be her birthday. May twenty-eight."

Garrett nodded. "She'll turn six?"

"Mhm. Why do you ask?"

He shrugged. "I was just wondering."

"When's your birthday?" Lucy asked.

"November twenty-six. I was born on Thanksgiving."

A smile curved Lucy's mouth. "That's special."

Garrett smiled. "My mother always thought so." He sent the last of his coffee down his throat then took the mug to the kitchen. "When do you turn eighteen?"

"The second of March."

"Ellen's birthday is March third."

"Wow. We're almost exactly a year apart then."

He nodded. "Between you and Travis, are you the older or younger?"

She smiled. "Younger. By forty-two minutes. Travis was actually born on the first of March. Just a few minutes before midnight."

"That probably doesn't happen very often."

Lucy shook her head. "First I'd ever heard of, though I don't really know of any other twins."

"I know of a couple sets, but they were both born on the same day."

"I guess we were just different." She smiled fondly before snapping out of her reverie with a yawn.

"Are you tired?"

Lucy opened her mouth to respond then yawned again. "I guess I am." She set her things aside and stood, stretching. "I should probably get some rest."

She waited for Garrett to rise. "Good night, Lucy." He grinned and leaned down to kiss her cheek.

She wondered when she should tell him that she was ready for a real kiss. That not only was she ready for one, she was sincerely wanting one. Probably tomorrow night, when Joan was at the Johnstons'. That might just be the perfect opportunity.

Lucy smiled. "Good night, Garrett."

Sixteen

Garrett could hardly concentrate all day. Since Joan was sleeping at the Johnstons', he and Lucy would be by themselves tonight. It could be the right time to tell her. To tell his wife that he was in love with her. Though he was nearly certain she felt the same way, his mind did its utmost to come up with the worst ways she could possibly respond. He also thought of some of the best ways she could respond too but a few times those ones led to a place he ought not to think on and he ended up with his face as red as a ripened tomato.

By the end of the day, he was almost nervous to enter his own house and found himself stopping for a deep breath before opening the door.

Lucy was setting the table when he entered the kitchen. She glanced up at him and smiled. "I hope you don't mind leftover butter beans and fried potatoes. There was enough for the two of us so I just warmed it up with some of the cornbread I made the other day."

Garrett nodded. "Sounds yummy."

"It'll be ready in just a minute if you want to wash up. I should have it out by the time you're done."

He nodded again and moved past her to wash his hands in the sink. He pumped water from the hand pump, listening to his wife prepare supper behind him.

Garrett could barely believe he was experiencing this. He had a sweet, kind, pretty wife who he could honestly say he was in love with, preparing a delicious meal for them to share together. The only way it could be better was if he turned around, lassoed that pretty little wife of his, and got a kiss, freely given. Hopefully, he wouldn't have to wait for that moment for too much longer.

He finally turned around and took his seat at the head of the table. Lucy joined at the seat to his left. Garrett made his mouth work. "My grandparents used to hold hands when they prayed. I've always liked the idea." He opened his palm on the table and Lucy's smaller hand fit into his.

They bowed their heads. "Dear God, thank You for this day and for this food which You have provided for us. I pray that You will help Joan to have fun at the Johnstons'. Please keep her safe and keep Lucy and I safe as well. And please let our conversation be pleasing to You. Amen." *And please give me the courage to tell Lucy that I love her. And please let her love me too.*

"Amen," Lucy echoed before slipping her hand out of his. She met his gaze with a smile. "Did you want holding hands while we pray to become a tradition or was that just for tonight?"

He shrugged. "I was thinking just for tonight but either is fine with me."

Lucy smiled, then took a bite of her food. Garrett followed her example and began to eat his supper.

"Did you let Miguel know he won't need to bring Joan to school tomorrow?"

Garrett nodded. "I did. Joan had already told him though."

"It figures. She really looks up to him."

"He enjoys her company. I think she reminds him that he has a child of his own." Garrett took another bite of the butter beans and chewed it before speaking again. "I think this tastes even better the second time."

"I agree. I'll have to remember that next time. I wonder if perhaps you made it but didn't eat it until the next day it would taste the same. Or maybe the flavor is enhanced because there's only a little of it left." She shrugged.

"I don't know, but feel free to experiment."

"You like it, don't you?"

Garrett nodded. "It's one of my favorites."

Lucy smiled. "Has Miguel found a cowhand yet?"

"No." He shook his head. "He's looked around and hasn't seen anyone that wants to work and knows how. Too bad Peter's boys aren't old enough."

"If they were, they'd probably be working with their pa."

"That's true." Garrett stared past Lucy for a second. "I just wish Amos didn't have to leave. He was a good worker."

"Well, I can certainly understand why he left. And I'm sure his wife is glad to have him home for their second child. It's not right for a man to be away from his family for so long."

"I know. I just wish I'd had more notice. I didn't expect him to be gone so suddenly. I do understand though."

"I don't think he ever should have left his wife in the first place, honestly," Lucy stated.

"Well, he felt like he had to. They needed the money and there wasn't any decent work available over there at the time. He never planned to be gone for long," Garrett defended the cowhand.

Lucy nodded. "Just until he had enough money saved to get back on his feet."

He nodded. "It's a good thing he decided to leave now though, while things are slow. We really don't need another hand yet, I just like to have all twelve available in case I need them."

"That's a wise idea."

His gaze settled on the still-slightly visible bruise on her collar bone. The color came out almost to her neck and when she was wearing a wide collar, as she was now, it was easy to see.

She noticed his look. "What?"

"It's still visible."

Lucy glanced down at it and waved a hand. "Don't worry about it. It's been fading. It's not quite as dark as it used to be. And I can't even feel it anymore."

"It still doesn't look very good."

"Just don't pay it any attention. It'll be gone before you know it." She looked at his empty plate. "Are you finished?"

"Yes. Thank you. It was delicious. You've caught on to cooking really well."

Lucy stood and started for the kitchen with their dishes. "I had a good teacher," she quipped with a wink.

Garrett grinned and helped her clear the table.

They washed their few dishes and quickly dried them and put them away. Within a few minutes, they were in the sitting room.

Garrett noticed that Lucy didn't reach for Joan's nearly-finished jacket. She stared into space to his left and then turned to him with a small smile.

"Do you ever just remember something all of a sudden? Like someone just put it in your mind and, for whatever reason, you're stuck thinking about it?"

"I think I have, once or twice. What do you remember?"

"It came to me this morning actually. I was six years old, I think, shortly before my mother died. My mother, father, Travis and I were all there by the fireplace and I went up to Pa and tried to tickle him. Travis and I tried before, on his stomach and sides, under his chin, the bottoms of his feet. We never could get a peep out of him. He never was ticklish and never would be, he always said. He liked it when we'd try and usually ended up tickling us instead. This time, I somehow thought to tickle him under his arms and he practically roared with laughter. Travis did his best to hold Pa down while I tickled him with all my strength. Pa was almost as weak as a newborn calf. He tried to fend us off but he was laughing so hard he could barely do anything. Ma just watched and cheered us on. We all laughed until we were crying." Lucy's countenance lit and though she was smiling, there was a sheen over her eyes.

"That's always been one of my favorite memories. I hope I never forget it."

Garrett smiled. "Me and my siblings used to have tickle wars. Nobody really ever won, but it was a lot of fun. Once in a while Pa joined in, but he always won. He'd hold two of us and the rest would attack the prisoners and make 'em laugh until they could hardly breathe. We all loved it. Haven't done it in a long time though."

Lucy stood suddenly and approached him. He caught the mischievous gleam in her eye.

"I'm not ticklish anymore," he warned. "I haven't been since I was a teenager. My sisters have already tried."

Lucy grinned and plopped onto the seat beside him. "I'm not your sister."

She reached for him and wiggled her fingers over his

sides. A sense of mirth rose in his throat but he fought it and simply smiled. *Could I really still be ticklish?*

"I told you I'm not ticklish anymore."

She grinned as though she knew he was lying, and continued relentlessly until he could no longer hold it back and chuckled. Lucy giggled in response. He caught her hand and held it away from him, trying to fight his laughter. She kept at him with her other hand and he attempted to ward her off.

Garrett poked his finger at her side and she twisted away. He grinned and did it again. She jumped to her feet, a giggle spilling out of her. He stood and she ran to the kitchen. He gave chase. She dashed around the table and back out into the sitting room, then into her bedroom. Garrett grabbed at her foot and barely missed as she scrambled over the bed. She squealed and raced back into the sitting room.

He caught her before she could escape back into the kitchen and tickled her. She squirmed and giggled and did her best to return the onslaught. They both roared with laughter and continued to tickle each other even though their vision blurred with tears.

Lucy eventually collapsed, giggling breathlessly. "Stop," she managed. "Stop for a moment."

Garrett obliged and they sat on the floor trying to contain their laughter and return their breathing to normal.

Lucy wiped away the moisture gathered in her eyes and leaned back on her arms. "That was fun," she said with a smile, her voice still a hint breathless.

He nodded and swallowed before responding. "Was? Are you done?" He gave her side a poke.

A chuckle spilled out as she batted his finger away. "For now, yes. Laughing always makes me so weak." She clasped her hands behind her head and lowered herself to the floor. Her eyes closed.

Garrett watched her as her stomach rose and fell with every inhale and exhale, her breathing slowly returning to normal. He fought the temptation to feel if her flushed cheeks were extra warm or if the pink was just there to look pretty.

She opened her eyes and saw him watching her. She smiled and sat up. "What are you thinking about?"

"How pretty you look with pink cheeks."

She dipped her head. "Thank you."

Should he tell her now? Anticipation began to build inside of him and he opened his mouth. "Lucy, I—"

"— Garrett—"

They both stopped.

The tips of her mouth rose slightly. "You go ahead."

"No, it's all right. Go on," he prompted.

"Well, I-I was gonna say that I.... Do you remember what we talked about earlier? A while ago? About... kissing?"

Garrett nodded.

"I'm ready. To, you know, start kissing for real. I'm more than ready." She smiled, trepidation and excitement in her face.

He swallowed hard and scooted closer. He reached

for her face and let his thumb rub her cheek. It was warm. And soft.

Lucy glanced down at his hand, then up into his eyes. "What do you want me to do?" she whispered.

"Just close your eyes."

She obeyed and Garrett lowered his mouth onto hers and tasted it. He felt a tremor course through Lucy and she raised a hand to his chest. He pulled back.

"How was that?"

She opened her eyes and licked her lips. She glanced at his mouth. "Can I have another one?"

His sentiments exactly. Garrett grinned and met her lips again. This time, Lucy's hand traveled up around his neck. She kissed him back and he deepened the kiss, letting his fingers delight in her soft hair as he did. A little sound came from her throat and a feeling of pleasure welled. He pulled her closer.

A sudden sharp sound broke them apart. Someone knocking on the door.

Lucy's face pinkened and Garrett felt heat climbing his own neck. They stared at each other for a minute before the knock sounded again.

Garrett stood and walked to the door, hearing Lucy rise behind him. He opened the door, instantly wary when he spotted a smaller, unfamiliar man. He cleared his throat. "What do you need?"

The man stiffened the second he saw him. "I'm looking for a girl named Lucille Weber. She's seventeen. Know of her?"

Garrett widened his stance. What could this man want with his wife? He wished it wasn't so dark, so he could see him better. "Yes, I do. Who are you?"

He felt Lucy approach from behind him and peek over his shoulder.

"Travis?"

Seventeen

Lucy's eyes widened in shock. "Travis? Is it you?" She tried to duck under Garrett's restraining arm, but he didn't let her through. She glanced up at him and he gave her a small shake of his head, suspicion darkening his face. Reason entered her mind. She hadn't seen her brother in over three years. It was possible that it wasn't him. But that voice.

Garrett turned back to the man. "Come inside." He stepped back and the other man entered the house. The light fell across his face and joy welled in Lucy's heart.

"Travis!" Tears pooled in her eyes as she launched herself into his arms.

He stumbled back a step, before steadying. His arms closed around her. "Lucy," his voice rasped in her hair. She knew the scratchiness of it meant he was fighting the urge to cry.

Travis was here! Her brother had found her! He'd come back for her! He could live with them and see

Joan again and work with Garrett. The thought of her husband made Lucy pause and pull back.

She looked to Garrett, whose gaze still held suspicions. She'd have to help him relieve that. She returned to Garrett's side. "Travis, this is my husband. Garrett, this is my brother."

Travis' eyes narrowed into slits as he eyed Garrett up and down for several seconds. His body held stiff, he met Lucy's gaze. "Can we speak alone for a minute?" he asked, glancing at Garrett with contempt.

Lucy nodded.

"I'm not sure I like that idea," Garrett spoke up. Travis glared bullets into Garrett. Tension cracked in the air.

Lucy turned to her husband. "It's okay, Garrett. Please. Just for a couple minutes. We can just talk in my bedroom." Her voice lowered. "He's my brother. He'd never harm me."

Garrett glanced at Travis, then back at her. He nodded slightly. "Three minutes. If he tries to lay a hand on you, yell. I don't trust him."

"Thank you," Lucy whispered. She didn't tell him that doubts of her brother's safety edged the back of her mind as well.

"Come, Travis. We can talk in here." She motioned to the bedroom door and he finally tore his glare away from Garrett and entered. She followed him and shut the door behind her.

Travis whirled toward her, his gaze intense in the

dim light coming through the window. "What has he done to you? Tell me now, Lucy."

She shook her head. "What do you mean? Garrett hasn't done anything to me."

He stepped closer to her and she took an involuntary step back. "Don't lie to me, Lucy. I know his type. They'll do anything to get what they want. Even abuse innocent people. I've seen it before. He's just like it. Big, strong enough to break bones with a single punch." He shuddered and ran a hand over his face.

Lucy shivered. What pain lay in Travis' past?

He turned desperate eyes to her. "What has he done to you? Tell me, Lucy. I'll protect you from him."

She shook her head again. "Nothing, Travis. Garrett isn't like that. He's kind and gentle. He'd never lay a hand on me." She rested her hand on his arm.

His eyes met with her collar bone and instantly hardened. "If he hasn't done anything to you, how did you get this?" He touched the bruise just above her collar.

"I fell. Garrett was teaching me how to ride a horse. She spooked and I fell and landed on my shoulder. I'm all better but the bruise hasn't gone away yet."

Travis shook his head. "I don't believe you. He told you to say that."

"No, he didn't, Travis. Garrett isn't like those other men you know. He'd never raise his hand against a woman, or anyone. He isn't like that at all."

"Even if he has never struck you, that doesn't mean he hasn't harmed you. How about…in other ways? There's more than one way to abuse a woman," he said quietly, seemingly haunted by memories.

"What do you mean?"

Travis swallowed hard. "Has he touched you? Has he…has he forced himself on you?"

Her heart throbbed at whatever Travis had seen while he was gone, whatever had put that fear into his mind. She shook her head. "Never. And he never would touch me without my consent. Garrett is a kind, God-fearing man, Travis. Whatever you're thinking he's done, he hasn't. He's been nothing but good to me."

"I don't know if I can believe that."

"Why? Travis, what happened? What happened while you were gone that would make you assume Garrett was capable of such things?"

"A man is capable of many wicked things, Lucy."

"But what happened to make you think that way? What did you see?"

He glanced past her, ignoring her questions. "Nothing. Nothing happened. I don't want to talk about it."

"But, Travis—"

"No," he cut her off. "Please. Don't ask."

She nodded and glanced at his lanky frame, suddenly noticing how skinny he was. "When was the last time you ate?"

He shook his head and looked away as though it didn't matter. "I had something yesterday."

Yesterday? No wonder her brother wasn't thinking rationally. He was half starved. "Come. I'll get you something to eat."

"No. Not now. I'd like to talk while we still can."

"Okay." They were silent for a moment. "How did you find me?"

"I tracked down the train and found out that you were gone. Mrs. Walton wouldn't tell me anything but one of the other kids said you got married in Saddle, Texas. So I came here and it wasn't long until I found out where you lived."

"Did they tell you that Joan is with me? Garrett adopted her too." Lucy smiled.

"The little girl you took care of?"

She nodded.

He shook his head. "I didn't know that."

"I don't know if she remembers you, but she'll be happy to see you. I'm happy to see you, Travis." Lucy stepped toward her brother and wrapped her arms around him, holding him close. She listened to his heartbeat as he gradually relaxed and returned her embrace. "I love you, Travis. I'm so glad you found me."

He sighed. "Me too." He pulled back and glanced furtively at the door before leaning down until their faces were an inch apart. "I want to take you away."

Her eyes widened. "What?"

His voice was a sharp whisper. "We can escape. Tonight or perhaps some other time. You can come and we can find a place and tough it out on our own, just like we did when Mother died. We can bring Joan too, if you want. You don't have to live here with him."

"I can't do that."

"Yes, you can. Don't be afraid of him. He won't know until we're halfway across the state."

"Travis, you don't understand. I don't want to run away. I have nothing to escape from. I love my life here and I...love Garrett too." Lucy realized the truth in her words as soon as they came out of her mouth. She truly did love her husband. With all her heart.

A barrage of emotions hit Travis in the face and he reeled. "Don't say that."

"Say what? That I love my husband?"

"That man..." A tremor shook her brother's shoulders and he turned his back to her. "Don't say that you love him. You don't know what that is. You're just confusing yourself. You can't love a man like that. You don't know what it will do to you. What it did to her." Travis' voice was low, like he was talking to himself, caught up in memories.

"What did it do to her?" Lucy asked softly.

Travis pivoted and met her gaze with torture-filled eyes. "It destroyed her."

Garrett knocked on the door. "Lucy?"

Lucy ignored her brother's glare at the door and went to open it. She smiled at her husband. "Thank you, Garrett, for letting us talk. Travis, come on, let's get you something to eat."

She quickly found some bread, butter, and jam and put it on the table, trying not to notice how Travis started eating as though he hadn't in days. She met Garrett's gaze with a pained smile, wondering just what her brother had gone through in the three years they'd been apart.

When her brother was finished, she put away the rest of the butter and jam and returned to Travis' side. Weariness seemed to weigh him down and he fought a yawn.

She set a hand on his arm. "You can sleep in my room tonight, Trav."

Travis' eyes flinted. He glanced at Garrett, then back at her. "And where will you sleep?"

She hadn't thought quite that far. Her gaze flitted to her husband but didn't quite meet his eyes. Warmth spread across her face. "Oh, I-I hadn't thought—"

"You can sleep in my room," Garrett offered.

Travis growled.

"I can sleep in the sitting room," Garrett finished, raising a brow in her brother's direction.

Travis met him stare for stare before breaking away and leaning down to whisper in her ear. "If he tries anything, scream and I'll come save you."

Lucy nodded for her brother's benefit and bid him good night. With one last glare at Garrett, Travis went into Lucy's room and shut the door.

Garrett started for his own bedroom and Lucy followed. He entered it and gathered a blanket.

"I'm sorry. I didn't mean to kick you out of your own room."

Garrett pivoted toward her, his eyes sharp. "What, precisely, did you mean?"

She realized how that must have sounded and blushed. "Well, I-I don't know. I suppose I didn't really think about it."

He studied her silently for a moment. Lucy felt peculiar, both of them standing in his room. It made her think of things she shouldn't.

"What did Travis say to you? You looked frightened when you came out."

"He-He's afraid of you…for me. He thinks you've done ridiculous things, that you abuse me and do unspeakable deeds. There is something in his past that he won't talk about. Whatever it was, it was horrible. He never acted like that before." She swiped at a tear that fell. "He is so afraid and bitter."

Garrett nodded. "I don't think whatever happened was very long ago. His wounds will most likely heal with time."

"What if they don't? He mentioned something… something about a girl and that she destroyed herself by loving a man. I don't know what he means. He doesn't want me to ask any questions."

"Hopefully he'll open up with time too. If he becomes at peace with his past, he will probably eventually share it with you."

Lucy approached her husband. "Garrett, do you

think he can stay on here? You need another cowhand and I'm sure Travis can learn. Please?"

He smiled. "Of course. He'll have to bunk with the other ranch hands and I don't know if I trust him yet, but he can stay. I knew you wouldn't want to part with him, now that you got your brother back."

Lucy flung her arms around him and gave him a squeeze. "Thank you."

Garrett's arms closed around her and held her to him for a moment. Then he freed her and set her away from him. He smiled. "Since it's time we go to sleep, I think I owe you a good night kiss."

Her head dipped for a second before she returned his gaze. "But, Garrett."

"Hm?"

"It doesn't have to be on my cheek. I think right here"—she tapped her lips—"is a better place." She grinned.

Garrett wasted no time and covered her smile with his lips. She wrapped her fingers around his neck to keep him close. His large hand covered the small of her back and drew her into him.

So many pleasant, warm thoughts ran through her mind, of her and Garrett and children. Garrett deepened the kiss and her senses soared. What she had said to Travis was true. She fully and truly loved her husband. For his kindness, his patience, his determination, his consideration for others. He was her hero and none of Travis' fears could change that.

Garrett broke away for a moment and she sucked in air as he nuzzled her neck. He returned to her mouth a moment later.

"Garrett," she said against his mouth.

"Hm?"

"I love you."

His head jerked away from hers so quickly she would have stumbled had he not been holding her.

He swallowed and his eyes searched hers. "You do?"

She nodded, hoping, praying he loved her in return. "I've been falling in love with you ever since we met. You're more than I ever dreamed of in a husband."

Garrett's green eyes gazed at her so tenderly her heart melted a little more. "I love you too, Lucy. I want to show you that I do every day I breathe."

Tears pricked her eyes and she blinked them away, burrowing her head into his chest. She sighed, too overcome with joy and love to do anything else. She basked in the moment before lifting her head and kissing Garrett. She pulled away a second later with a smile. He leaned down to kiss her again, this time a long, achingly beautiful one.

"We better go to bed. I mean, I should go to sleep. Out there." He kissed her once more, quickly. "Before I can't."

She opened her eyes and nodded, smiling. "You should." She kissed him again. "Good night," she murmured against his lips.

"Good night, Lucy." He kissed her forehead and then left as swiftly as possible, shutting the bedroom door behind him.

Lucy lowered herself onto Garrett's bed, inhaling his scent. A giggle rose in her throat, quickly followed by a sigh. Her fingers rose to touch her lips. What would happen now?

Eighteen

Garrett awoke before dawn as usual, and made good use of the time he took to pray after reading his Bible.

His mind immediately went to his wife. *Thank You, Lord, for blessing me with Lucy. Thank You for giving her a love in her heart for me and thank You for giving me a love for her as well. Thank You for last night and all that went well.* Their conversation the night before was still fresh in his mind. His lips curved into a smile as he forced himself out of his daydreams threatening to carry him away. *Please bless our relationship and let it develop into a real marriage.*

A sound came from Lucy and Joan's bedroom and he remembered their visitor from the night before – his brother-in-law. *I pray that You will give us strength and wisdom and patience for all that we'll face with Travis and his past. Please help him to let go of his bitterness and find healing in You, Lord. Help us all.*

Garrett looked up when the door to his bedroom

opened quietly. Lucy, dressed for the day with her hair up in a tidy bun, smiled at him, stepping forward out of his room.

"Did you sleep well?" he heard himself say.

She nodded with a shy smile. "I did. You have a comfortable bed."

He decided not to dwell on that thought and stood, closing his Bible and setting it down on the small table beside the couch.

"What do you want for breakfast?" his wife asked, heading for the kitchen.

He shrugged and followed her. "It doesn't matter to me. Just something to eat."

She checked on the wood stove's furnace, which he had started after he woke up to stave off some of the cold, before setting a frying pan on it. "How about eggs, fried potatoes, and sausage scramble with toast?"

He grinned and leaned toward her, memories of kisses from yesterday tantalizing his mind. "Sounds delicious."

She tossed him a smile over her shoulder and started cracking eggs into a bowl. He made himself useful and found the potatoes. He washed six of them and began chopping them into little cubes.

They worked in silence for a moment before Lucy spoke up. "About last night, Garrett."

He turned to her. "Yes?"

"I, um, really enjoyed it. Feel free to kiss me anytime."

He smiled, abandoning his potatoes and wrapping an arm around her waist, drawing her nearer. "Anytime, huh?"

Her gaze flickered from his eyes to his mouth. "Mm-hmm."

The door to Lucy and Joan's bedroom opened before their lips met. Garrett released his wife and met Travis' disgusted look. His brother-in-law ignored Lucy's cheerful greeting and stormed outside.

Lucy started after her brother. "You don't think he's leaving, do you?"

Garrett shook his head. "No. He isn't. He wouldn't leave without you."

"He's not leaving with me, either. I'm not going anywhere."

Garrett looked to his wife, her hands planted firmly on her hips as though she expected Travis to hear her and come back inside to argue her statement. "I'm glad to hear that."

She turned toward him and then glanced at the sausage beginning to sizzle on the stove. She hurried past him to it and moved it around with a wooden spoon before adding his potatoes. "Do you suppose he'll leave once he realizes that?" Her eyes met his, damp with emotion.

"I don't think so. I doubt he'd search for you for so long and then just give up once he found you. If nothing else, I'm sure he'll stay to protect you."

"But I don't need his protection." She sighed. "How

long do you think it will take for him to see that too? To realize that everything isn't the same as it was in his past?"

"That's all up to Travis. Whenever he lets go of his anger and bitterness and lets God heal him. It could be today, or he could hold on to it for years. It's all up to him."

Garrett watched as Lucy turned back to their breakfast and retrieved a loaf of bread, placing it in the oven to warm. "It's hard to believe it was just yesterday that Joan skipped off to school, ready to spend the night at the Johnstons'."

He nodded and took a step toward his beautiful wife. "Or that it was just yesterday that you attacked me with your squirming fingers?" He reached for her and prodded her side with his index finger.

She caught his finger and grinned. "Would you like to do that again?"

He dropped a kiss onto her forehead. "Better not. I'm sure your brother would get the wrong idea if he saw me chasing you."

"I'm sure he'd get the right idea if he saw me kissing you."

He smiled as his hand found her waist. "And what idea is that?"

"That I love you."

He raised his eyebrows, feigning surprise. "Oh, you do?"

"Yes, I do. Now hurry up and kiss me before I have to get back to breakfast."

Garrett laughed and obeyed, making sure his demanding little wife was more than satisfied.

By the time Joan returned from school, Lucy had decided the day had gone pretty well. Travis had been civil to Garrett, in her presence at least, and she had simply done as she usually did, though she couldn't remember a day in which she smiled and sighed so much. Marriage truly was a beautiful thing. Thinking back on her time on the orphan train, remembering old fears, she could hardly believe she lived the life she now lived. There were no words to describe how blessed she was.

"Did you have a good time at the Johnstons'?" Lucy asked as Joan came skipping toward her.

She nodded adamantly. "Yes, Mama, I did. Rose said it was warm enough so we went swimmin' and I played with Hope's doll and had lots and lots of fun!" She beamed. "Can I do it again? Please?"

"Someday you can, but not today. Why don't you go put your things inside?"

"I will!" She ran up to the door and then stopped just before opening it. "Mama, who's that man out there talkin' to Mr. Miguel?"

Lucy smiled. "That's someone I'd like you to meet. Hurry up and put your slate and pail away."

Joan quickly obeyed and was back out in a flash. She grabbed Lucy's hand. "Let's go!"

Lucy let Joan pull her toward the corral, where the

two men were talking. Her heart warmed at the sight of her brother. It was so wonderful to have him with her again. If only he were the same as she remembered him. *Dear God, please heal Travis.*

When Miguel spotted them approaching, he said something to Travis and turned to leave, tipping his hat respectfully to Lucy and giving Joan a small smile.

Lucy squatted next to Joan. "Travis, this is Joan. Joan, this is Travis. He's my brother. Do you remember him from the orphan train? He was on there too but he left just a little bit after you came."

Joan shook her head. "I don't 'member him."

"That's all right. Travis was looking for me and he found me here last night. So if it's okay with him, he's gonna stay on here for a while and work with Mr. Miguel and the other ranch hands." Lucy glanced up at her brother, who scowled.

"I don't know if I like him, Mama. He don't look very nice," Joan whispered, her eyes worried.

"Just wait until you get to know him some." Lucy smiled. "You can go talk to Mr. Miguel now if you want."

Joan beamed. "Thank you, Mama!" She pecked her cheek and took off for the barn.

"Just make sure you don't disturb him if he's working," Lucy called after her. She stood and met her brother's gaze.

"She calls you 'Mama'," he noted aloud.

She nodded. "I'm the only mother she's ever known."

Travis didn't comment.

"Did Garrett talk to you about staying on and bunking with the ranch hands?"

The scowl was back. "He did."

She placed a hand on his arm. "I hope you'll stay, Travis. I don't want to lose my brother again."

"I'll stay for now, to make sure you're safe."

"Then I hope while you're here, you see that I am safe, safer than I've ever been. And happier than I've ever been."

Travis looked away.

"You can be happy again too, Travis. Let God heal you and—"

"Stop, Lucy. Don't talk to me about God. He doesn't care." Travis glared, anger evident in his voice.

"But—"

"I know I once thought He did, but I was wrong."

"But, Travis—"

"I have to go, Lucy. I'm sure Garrett has some chores for me to do." He left her and marched toward the barn. Lucy wanted to chase after him, but she didn't.

"Oh, God, heal his heart," she prayed.

Nineteen

Garrett's jaw tightened. "Are you sure?"

Miguel nodded in affirmation. "Forty head are missing. Sam saw tracks from two unfamiliar horses. He followed them a little ways before they disappeared."

"I'll ride out after breakfast. You and Sam can join me."

The foreman's head dipped in a nearly imperceptible nod.

They both glanced at the bunkhouse as Travis came out.

Garrett studied his foreman. "You don't suspect him, do you?"

Miguel shook his head. "But I will watch him."

"Thank you. Have the horses ready in thirty minutes."

Miguel nodded and Garrett strode toward the house.

"Good morning." Lucy smiled at him from the stove. She held a wooden spoon.

Garrett attempted to push his worries aside as he

greeted his wife. "Good morning, Mrs. Black." She turned to him and he gave her a kiss. "Is breakfast ready?"

"Mm-hmm. I made oatmeal."

"It smells delicious."

"Hopefully your nose and taste buds are in agreement then." She smiled and retrieved the pot, before setting it on the table.

Joan was at the table already, eating a buttered slice of bread.

"Joan! You aren't supposed to start eating without us," Lucy admonished.

"But I already prayed, Mama. And I gotta hurry, 'cuz Mr. Miguel's waiting to take me to school."

"Miguel won't be able to take you to school today, Joan. You'll have to have Mama take you today."

Lucy frowned, clearly puzzled. "Why is that, Garrett?"

"I'm going to need Miguel this morning. I can tell you about it later." He glanced surreptitiously at Joan.

Understanding lit Lucy's eyes. "Should we pray and eat then?"

Garrett nodded and they all bowed their heads. "Dear God, thank You for this food. Please bless it and bless us all. Help us to follow You and do what is right. In Your name, amen."

They began eating their breakfast.

"Did you see Travis out there?" Lucy asked.

Garrett nodded around a mouthful.

"I'm guessing he's eating with the rest of the cowhands?

I wasn't sure whether I should set him a place or not."

"He'll take his meals with the ranch hands in the bunkhouse."

She agreed with a small nod.

Joan jumped up with her empty bowl. "I'm all done, Mama! Can we go?"

"Take your dishes to the kitchen first and then get all your things. I'll still be a little while. You can wait for me out on the porch, okay?"

"Okay." Joan brought her bowl and spoon to the kitchen and then collected her slate and lunch pail and headed for the door. "Don't take too long, Mama."

"I'll do my best."

Joan shut the door and Lucy immediately turned to him. "What's happening?"

"Forty head of cattle are missing. Sam just discovered it this morning."

She gasped.

"Miguel, Sam, and I are gonna ride out and try to find some clues."

"Be careful."

"We will. Don't worry about it."

"I'll try not to." She glanced down at her breakfast. "Do you have any suspicions?"

"I do."

"You don't think it was Travis, do you?"

Garrett shook his head. "No. He doesn't know his way around cattle and I doubt he has the money to hire someone else to help him."

She nodded. "Then…you don't think it could be Clem, do you?" Lucy rubbed her arms in a comforting gesture.

"I don't know. He's the only person I can think of that has anything against me, but I can't be sure." Garrett stood and crouched beside her chair. "Don't be afraid of him, Lucy. If he dares come near you again, I'll take care of him once and for all. I won't let him scare you again."

"Thank you, Garrett," she whispered. "I love you."

"I love you too." Garrett stood and Lucy followed him, wrapping her arms around him and resting her head on his chest. He wondered if she could hear the thumping of his heartbeat. "I would feel better if you took Travis with you to the Johnstons'."

She nodded and pulled back enough to look up at him. "We should probably go soon. I don't want Joan to be late for school."

"Take some horses with you. Hopefully Miguel and I will be back in time so he can bring her home from school."

Lucy pulled his head down and kissed him. "Be safe."

Once Joan was safely at school and she and Travis were riding back home, Lucy glanced at her brother. She wondered if she'd ever be able to find out what happened while he was gone. If only he'd tell her. Then she could try to help him, would know how to help him.

Travis' voice reached her ears. "What are you thinking about?"

Lucy focused. "I'm wondering what could have happened while you were gone."

He sighed. "I can't tell you, Lucy. You wouldn't want to know."

Her heart broke at the pain in his voice. "But I do, Travis. I want to help you. I want you to be happy."

Travis stared at the reins in his hands. "Maybe someday, Lucy. Maybe someday I can tell you. But not now. Don't ask me now."

"All right. I won't." They rode on in silence. Lucy enjoyed the now-comfortable rhythm of Autumn's steady gait beneath her. It reminded her of the many riding lessons she'd had.

"Okay, Lucy, today you're going to ride Autumn. We'll ride around for a while so you can get accustomed to her gait before we graduate to a trot."

Garrett let her mount the horse on her own before he swung up unto his horse. "You know how to hold the reins. Loose, but not with too much slack. Give her a kick to get her started."

Lucy nodded and firmly nudged Autumn in the side. The horse began walking and Garrett rode his mount abreast of her.

"When you're comfortable on her, squeeze your legs and ease her into a trot."

Lucy walked the horse for a while before she worked up the courage to follow his instructions. "Come on, Autumn, let's go."

She squeezed her legs and Autumn picked up speed, her walk quickly evolving into a trot. Her heartbeat immediately kicked up. It took Lucy a little while before she stopped bouncing and was able to move in unison with the horse.

"Mama, you're trotting!" Joan clapped from her perch on the fence.

"I am!" Lucy grinned as her heartrate slowly calmed and her fear vanished.

Garrett followed her on his horse. "Beautiful, Lucy. That's perfect. You really are a good rider."

Lucy smiled at her husband and then laughed. Overcoming fear was an amazing feeling.

Rapid hoofbeats brought Lucy's mind back to the current moment. Autumn stopped suddenly and released a distressed whinny as another horse and rider blocked the trail. Her senses instantly alert, Lucy tried to recognize the man but couldn't.

His mustache curved with his mouth as he smiled. "Well, what've we got here?"

"What do you bet she's who Clem's been talkin' about, Skaggs?" Lucy turned to find another man, this one round and unsteady, blocking the road behind them. Skaggs. That name sounded familiar.

"Not a dime. Who do you reckon this fella is?" Skaggs tipped his head toward Travis, whose jaw tightened in what Lucy suspected was a combination of anger and fear.

"Don't know. Guess we could find out. Who are you?" the fat man asked Travis.

"No one you would know."

The man laughed. "He's a brave one, Skaggs." He turned to her brother. "Well then what are you doing with the pretty little lady here, hm?" Travis didn't answer and the outlaw turned to her. "How about you then? What's your name, miss?"

Lucy opened her mouth to speak but nothing came out. Should she say who she was? Should she invent a name or perhaps claim to be someone else, like Marie Johnston? Or would they already know who Marie was and call her on her bluff?

"Ain't got time for your games, missy. Answer me!" The man apparently had a short temper. He pulled out his pistol.

"Put it away, Lew. You're frightening the poor girl." Skaggs rolled his eyes. "You men around here have no idea how to treat women." He looked to Lucy. "Please tell us your name, dear."

"My…My name is Anna Rice. I'm traveling to San Antonio with my brother. Please let us by." She fought to keep her expression as innocent as possible.

Lew cackled behind her. "You've got Circle B markings on your horse. Looks to me like you're Lucy Black, miss, unless you're a horse thief."

Lucy shut her eyes. How stupid of her to forget.

"I don't believe she's a horse thief," Skaggs agreed with a smirk. "We'll bring them to Clem."

Twenty

By the time they had thoroughly searched for any traces of the missing cattle and had come up empty, Garrett was frustrated, cold, and starving. He, Miguel, and Sam rode home in silence, each contemplating the mystery. He had explained his suspicions to the men as they looked so each of them would be ready.

Garrett looked forward to finding Lucy waiting for him inside with a warm lunch and a sweet kiss. He woodenly dismounted at the barn and began relieving his horse of its saddle. He headed for the tack room and glanced toward the stalls. Why were they empty?

"Billy!"

The young ranch hand approached. "Yes, Boss?"

"Where are the other horses, Autumn and Travis' horse?"

He shrugged. "I don't know. I haven't seen them since this morning."

Something that pulsed like fear seeped into Garrett's

veins. "You mean, Mrs. Black and Travis haven't returned?"

"No, sir."

Garrett turned and marched back to his horse, slinging the saddle back onto it the instant he reached it. It was a trap. The whole thing had been a trap for Garrett to leave Lucy without protection. And he had played right into it like a fool. How stupid! He cinched the saddle, his fingers fumbling clumsily at his speed, and swung up onto his horse. He met his partners just outside of the barn. "Miguel, Sam, we're not finished. Travis and Lucy haven't returned."

"We will find them," Miguel said.

Garrett started off in the direction of the Johnstons' and heard them join him. He followed the horse's trail to the school, all the while fervently praying for Lucy's protection. *Oh God, keep her safe. Don't let Clem or anyone else hurt her.* They were almost to the Johnstons' place when he paused. He dismounted and studied the ground. "There was another rider."

Sam continued ahead of him. "Two of them. Looks like they were here returning to the ranch when two riders surrounded them."

Garrett nodded. "They headed this way." A trail of hooves headed eastward, off of the road between his and the Johnstons' ranch. "Let's go."

Lucy eyed the abandoned barn Skaggs and Lew led them to. It looked completely deserted. She prayed

Clem wouldn't be inside waiting. There was no telling what he would do to her without Garrett around. *God, please help us. Send Garrett, send anyone.*

Skaggs kept his pistol trained on her as he dismounted. "Go ahead and step down, dear." She did as she was told, watching as Lew and Travis did the same. They headed for the barn.

"Hey, Clem! Think I've got someone you'd be interested in." Lew grabbed her by the arm and pulled her into the barn. It took her eyes a moment before they adjusted to the dim light.

Clem stepped toward them with a smile, his gaze never leaving her face. She shivered. "I knew I'd have you one day. It took a bit of time but that doesn't matter. Not now that you're here." Clem reached for her face, then suddenly stopped. "Who is he?"

Skaggs trained his gun on Travis as Lew talked. "He was with her when we found 'em. They'd brought the little girl to school, just like you said."

"Well, I don't want anything to do with him. I just wanted the girl."

"You can't have her!" Travis spat. He jumped at Clem and knocked him to the ground. Lew rushed for them but Lucy stuck out her foot and he fell hard. A gunshot rent the air before anyone could go any further.

Skaggs waved his gun between her and Travis. "Don't move or I'll shoot. Lew, get off the floor. Tie him up."

The other man picked himself up off the floor and bound Travis' hands behind his back. Her brother glared bullets.

Clem stood, sporting a reddening eye. He spit dirt onto the barn floor and approached Travis, seething. "Thought you could get away with that?"

"The black eye looks good on you," Travis quipped.

Clem growled and slammed a fist into his jaw.

"Stop it!" Lucy ran at Clem and grabbed at his arm.

He jerked away and yanked her arms behind her, keeping her from hitting him.

Travis' face tightened in anger, despite the coloring along his mouth. "You leave her alone!"

Clem smirked as Travis struggled helplessly. "Gag him. And bind his legs too."

Lew obeyed, obviously happy to take part in Clem's plan.

"You two keep watch outside," Clem ordered. "I wouldn't be surprised if Black showed up lookin' for his wife." He leered down at Lucy. "You can come with me." He pushed Lucy in front of him, forcing her to a different area of the barn. She felt panic building in her throat. *Oh God, help me please. Don't let him touch me.* The thought of Clem stealing the sacred gift she had never shared with her husband made her want to sink to her knees and weep.

He released her. "Finally, we can get more acquainted." He caged her face in his hand and brought his mouth down on hers.

She struggled and stomped on his foot with all her strength.

He pulled away and swore. "I'll get you!" He slapped her and she slapped him back. His eyes narrowed in fury. "I don't think you understand this, missy. Anything you do will only make this worse. There is nothing you can do to stop me." To prove his point, Clem shoved her backward, making her trip over her skirts and fall. He stood over her. "Do you really think you're stronger than me? It'd be much easier if you wanted it too."

Lucy knew she needed time. "Garrett will find you and kill you. You won't get away with anything, Clem."

He smiled. "What makes you so sure he can find me? A dead man can't search for anyone."

"He isn't dead."

"Maybe not yet, but he will be. He'll get what's coming to him."

"So will you, Clem. One day you'll stand before God and He isn't gonna let you get away with anything."

"You just hush up! I'm tired of your jabbering."

He reached for her and she grabbed his arm and yanked him down. He fell toward her and she rolled. She jumped on him and pounded her fists into his face. He roared and grabbed at her hands. She struggled with him and did her best to keep him from her. He finally gained control of her hands and twisted to the side, pushing her off of him and onto the ground. She kicked at his legs until he trapped them between his own.

"I've had it with you, missy. It's time you pay."

"Where are they going?" Garrett wondered aloud as they followed the trail left by the four horses.

"My guess is to that abandoned barn at the edge of Skaggs' property. You remember it?"

"The one that should've fallen down years ago?"

Sam nodded.

The tracks continued leading them in the direction of the barn. Once they were near enough, the three men dismounted and headed toward the building on foot. They soon found it. "There are the horses."

"A man on both sides." Miguel pointed to the two men.

"That one looks like Skaggs," Sam noted.

Garrett studied the two entrances to the barn. "Sam, you keep an eye on things from here. Miguel and I will go around to the other side and enter through there. This man doesn't look nearly alert as Skaggs."

The cowhand nodded and Garrett and his foreman snuck their way around the barn, making sure they stayed out of view of the two men. When they reached the point they needed, they drew their pistols. "Miguel, keep going another thirty feet. I want to come at him from two different points, make him feel surrounded."

Miguel dipped his chin once in acknowledgement and continued through the rock and brush.

"God, please help us," Garrett whispered.

He stepped out into the open and advanced toward

the man, spying Miguel doing the same from the corner of his eye. It took a minute for the fat man to notice and he reached for his gun. Garrett leveled his pistol at the man's head. "Don't even try."

Miguel approached the man from behind and brought the butt of his gun down on his head. He fell with a grunt.

Footsteps sounded from the side of the barn. "Lew?" Skaggs.

Miguel nodded for Garrett to go inside and he quickly did, leaving his foreman to take care of the other man.

The first thing he saw was Travis, bound hand and foot and looking as though he had just worked off his gag. Travis' eyes were wild and desperate. "Clem has Lucy." Garrett tossed him his knife and hurried in the direction Travis indicated. A yell came from a horse stall and he headed for it.

Clem's voice reached his ears. "I've had it with you, missy. It's time you pay."

Rage roared in Garrett's ears as he took in the sight of his wife on the ground with Clem on top of her. He holstered his gun, grabbed Clem by the back of his shirt, and slammed a fist into his face. Clem scrambled to fight back but was no match for Garrett's righteous anger. He picked Clem off the floor to release some more of his fury when he heard a gun click beside him.

"That's enough, Garrett." Travis held a pistol in his hands, aimed at Clem's skull. "I can take care of him."

"Travis, don't." Lucy approached her brother. "Let the law take care of him."

Travis shook his head, the gun trembling in his hands. "He deserves it for what he did to you, and what he almost did to you."

Garrett was inclined to agree, especially seeing the pink hand print across her face – the one he was positive would fit Clem's hand.

"He does deserve it, Travis, I know he does. I know more than you do." She set a hand on her brother's arm. "But you don't, Travis. You don't deserve the scar killing a man will put on your soul. Let him have a trial, let them do whatever they decide to do to him. But it's not for you, Travis. Please."

Slowly, Travis lowered his gun.

Garrett spoke up. "Travis, you wanna truss him up? I'm sure there's some rope around here somewhere. And don't hesitate to use force if he doesn't listen."

Travis nodded and grabbed Clem, pushing him in front of him out into the other room.

Lucy was in his arms the second they left. Garrett held her and stroked her hair, praying she wasn't hurt any more than she seemed. What had Clem done in the time he was gone? "Lucy? Are you all right?"

She leaned back to look at him, tears in her eyes. "I'm fine. He didn't hurt me, other then what you see at least. I actually enjoyed pummeling him some." She sniffed. "Thank you for coming when you did."

"I would have come sooner if I could."

She shook her head. "I wish you did, but I think maybe you weren't supposed to."

"What do you mean?"

"I think I found some courage today. Before I-I was too scared to do anything, but today I fought back every moment I could. It's because of you. Because I have someone who I love that loves me too and what Clem was trying to take wasn't his but yours, my husband's." Her green eyes shone with tears as she smiled up at him.

Garrett leaned down and kissed her gently. Her hands found his neck and held him there as she kissed him back. When they finally pulled apart, warmth emanated from every part of him. He glanced away from his beautiful wife to find Travis standing outside of the stall, eyeing him with new respect in his gaze.

"Clem's ready to go and Miguel and Sam brought Lew and Skaggs in."

"Good. You, Miguel, and Sam can take the three of them to the sheriff in Saddle. Lucy and I have some things we need to take care of."

Travis left quietly.

"Things to take care of?" Lucy smiled.

He nodded. "What do you say, we go tell Joan she can stay the night at the Johnstons' again?"

His wife grinned and wrapped her arms around his neck, bringing him down for another kiss. "I think that's a wonderful idea."

Epilogue

Christmas Eve

"Mama! Quit kissin' Pa! You're gonna make him burn the turkey!" Joan shook her head at them in exasperation.

Lucy laughed and met Garrett's eyes. "Think we should listen to her?"

"She's right – the turkey will burn if we don't take care of it. But, truth be told, I'd rather be kissing you." Garrett smiled and leaned down to meet her lips again.

Joan groaned and they broke apart, laughing.

A few moments later, Garrett brought the turkey to the table and set it down. Lucy found her brother in the sitting room. "Travis, supper's ready. Are you coming?"

Travis turned to her. "I'm coming."

The four of them took their seats at the table and Garrett blessed the meal. "Dear God, thank You for sending Your Son to Earth to be born in a manger all those years ago. And thank You for a delicious meal and a wonderful family to share it with. Please bless this food and bless this evening. In Your name, amen."

"Amen," they echoed before helping themselves to the food.

"Mama," Joan spoke around her green beans. "Are we gonna go see Hope tomorrow?"

"Don't speak when your mouth is full, Joan. And yes, the Johnstons invited us over for Christmas supper." Lucy glanced at her twin. "Rose made sure to include you in that invitation too, Travis."

He nodded and smiled. "I would enjoy that."

Lucy was pleased to see the grip of her brother's past lessening in the way he interacted with others. She hoped healing wouldn't be too far off.

"I have a feeling we'll be eating this turkey the next week or two." Garrett eyed the bird. "It would be impossible for us to eat it all tonight."

Lucy agreed. "I'm sure I can think of some uses for it."

"Are we gonna have hot apple cider tonight, Mama? Please?" Joan begged.

She nodded. "Yes, Joan. Once we're finished eating, I'm gonna make some for us to drink while Pa reads us the Christmas story."

A half hour later, Joan cuddled close to Lucy on the couch as Garrett narrated the most beautiful story ever heard. Listening to her husband's voice and stroking her daughter's hair, Lucy settled her hand on her stomach, where she suspected her and Garrett's first baby rested, and sighed in contentment. God truly was good.

THE END

Reader reviews are oftentimes a determining factor in whether a reader will purchase a book or not. This is great help to authors and readers alike. If you enjoyed reading *The Orphan Bride*, please let me know what you thought of it. Your opinion is appreciated immensely! Thank you.

OTHER TITLES BY
BLESSED PUBLISHING ©

An Unforgivable Secret (Amish Secrets Book 1) by
J.E.B. Spredemann – http://amzn.to/1AqfteF

A Christmas to Remember by Michelynn Christy –
http://bitly.com/1KJtk3j

Coloring the Scriptures (An Alphabet Primer) by
Blessed Publishing – http://amzn.to/2cju8F0

ABOUT THE AUTHOR

Once upon a time, there was a little girl who loved to read. She read anything from horse mysteries to Christian romance. And she read a lot! As in, every spare second she had, when she wasn't playing with her siblings, was spent reading.

So, naturally, as the little girl grew up and began to ponder stories of her own, she did what any determined person would do and tried to write a story for herself. First she started out co-authoring (ten books!) with her mother and sister. But eventually, she branched out on her own.

That girl is me and that step led to the creation of my first novel, *The Orphan Bride*. My goal in writing is to touch your heart in some special way and to glorify Jesus Christ, my Lord and Saviour.

www.ingramcontent.com/pod-product-compliance
Lightning Source LLC
Chambersburg PA
CBHW051249250626
47155CB00009B/3225